Jo Barney
thank you!

JO BARNEY

outskirts press

Hat Trick

v2.0

This is a work of fiction. Names, characters, businesses, places, events, locales, and incidents are either the products of the author's imagination or used in a fictitious manner. Any resemblance to actual persons, living or dead, or actual events is purely coincidental.

The opinions expressed in this manuscript are solely the opinions of the author and do not represent the opinions or thoughts of the publisher. The author has represented and warranted full ownership and/or legal right to publish all the materials in this book.

Outskirts Press, Inc.
http://www.outskirtspress.com

ISBN: 978-1-9772-2692-1

PRINTED IN THE UNITED STATES OF AMERICA

CHAPTER ONE

"Shit! What do I do now?" I turned to my sister crouching behind me, the heels of her shoes digging into the mud to keep her from sliding down the bank and into me.

"What?" Sharon couldn't see what I could see because she was wiping her eyes on the collar of her jacket.

"Mom's not sinking. She's floating."

"This was such a stupid idea." Sharon's one free hand flailed out across the grass, the black dirt, the stolid water.

My feet sank deeper into the mud. "Give me something to stir her up with." I reached back, fingers waggling. Sharon slapped my hand with a long stiff piece of weed, and I leaned out over the brown water and stirred my mother into the Columbia slough.

I heard Sharon's moan and sucking sounds as she freed her feet, one at a time, and headed back up the slope. After a moment, I followed her, my Nikes threatening to stay behind with Mom.

My sister slumped and sat down on the edge of the bank a few feet above me, her white trousers seeping red mud around the edges of her butt, her eyes seeping red, too. She held out a hand and pulled me up to her side, and we looked over the still wet scene, two bereaved orphans.

A whoosh startled us, made us both gasp. Wings flapping, a blue heron rose like a Greek myth into the receiving sky, flicks of water tracing its path.

"Shit," I said. Mom had the last word again.

My mother had died the way she lived, without a lot of fuss. One week she was holed up, writing whatever she was thinking about at the time, little essays that she sent out and most of the time got back. The next week she was gone.

She had called on Sunday, asking how my week had gone. I told her fine, like I always did, and she said, "Fine, too," when I thought to ask about hers. The usual. We skimmed each other's lives with a few more questions and then said Love You and hung up before I remembered to ask her for the fifty bucks I needed to get me to my next unemployment check.

A week later, a doctor at St. Vincent's Hospital was on the phone telling me she was dying. I should come soon. By the time I got to her room, she could barely whisper my name and twitch a smile, her eyes, the part of her I still knew, the rest of her, white, folded into the sheets, a small, faint shadow. A nurse brushed by me, pressed on a tube, glanced at the beeping monitor and then back at me. Why weren't you around when she needed you? her narrow squint wondered.

My sister, sitting beside the bed, gave me the same look. "Did you know about this?" she asked, meaning that Mom hadn't told her either, that she was sick, about to die. For a minute, I felt a little better, then my mother jerked and whimpered a sigh.

I tried to think of words that would make my sister stop glaring at me, would let the nurse know that I wasn't that bad a son. Something about love, I supposed, but my mother already knew I loved her. Always had, no matter what. I leaned down to her and kissed her, and my lips left a dent in her soft cheek. "I'll be back." Then I pushed my way past the door and into the gray sick smell of the hall.

"Sure," my sister hissed at me, letting me know I was doing it again--leaving her to handle the hard stuff.

Outside, a gasp of fresh air stung my eyelids, made my eyes water.

"Disappointed," my parents used to call it, trying to name the source of my floods of childish tears. I got disappointed a lot as a kid. My howls agitated entire supermarkets and rang out above recorded carols on Christmas tree lots, destroyed a number of birthday parties. I got used to being carried from places headfirst, wedged under an armpit.

Then, at age seven, I took my first ice hockey lesson, and the disconsolate head of steam that percolated inside me found a way to vent. My sharp, shiney blades bit into the ice, obeyed me. My stick and I became one. I pummeled my opponents; I slammed pucks against and across padded bodies and into nets. And I learned, in my first real tournament, that hockey players, even when very disappointed, didn't cry, at least so that anyone noticed, not if they didn't want to be called Girly or Boo Hoo or worse. Even when the puck got away, flung itself into the wrong net, gave up the game, I learned to blink fast and look for a guy to mash into the boards.

However, in the hospital parking lot, as I blinked and pulled up the neck of my T-shirt to wipe my nose, no one was around to beat up. Asphalt, shiny with rain, stretched out in front of me and I stepped around puddles and clogged drains and headed to who knows where. A rush of water stopped me at a curb. Or maybe I stopped myself. Then I turned around and managed to make it back in time to say goodbye to my mother, Sharon crying, me blinking until I just shut my eyes.

The day after she died, my sister and I went to Mom's house to check on things. This was not Our House. It was the house Mom rented after she and Dad split. Our House had been sold to a young couple with twins, glad for the finished basement, ignorant of the dry rot in the attic. My father had bought a condo with his half of the equity, and Mom had stashed hers, deciding that renting a house with an extra bedroom for whatever kid might come home would leave her with enough to retire on and to write when the time came. The bungalow suited her with its small rooms, dark wood, familiar overstuffed furniture. On my several retreats from youthful forays into the real world, I had felt safe in that house, closeted behind its squeaky pocket doors.

That first day, Sharon wiped off the kitchen counters, made sure the oven was off, the refrigerator emptied of food that would be garbage before we made it back a week later. I rattled windows, double-locked the back door, turned off the furnace. Neither of us talked much, just did what had to be done.

Then, in her organized way, Sharon took a paper out of her pocket and read the schedule for the next week. First, the memorial service, Sharon reminded me, not funeral, maybe to make herself feel better. Then Mom would be scattered. She hadn't wanted to settle in one place forever, Sharon said, and we would make a day of it. Then the rental house had to be emptied. I wasn't working, so I would be in charge of that job. She, of course, would help, in between the times her husband and kids needed her. Apparently instead of blinking, my sister made lists.

Sharon and I weren't close. Ever. The trouble was that Sharon was always right, ever since we were little kids. And I was always wrong. By high school, I was living down to my sister's predictions and driving Mom crazy with worry, not that she gave up on me, despite Sharon's curled lip whenever she glanced at me over the dinner table. The lip relaxed a little after she got married and had other people to straighten out.

That first visit to Mom's house, neither one of us, in our separate states of sadness, noticed the yellow Post-it stuck to the screen of the iMac in her workroom.

The memorial service was held at the Unitarian church, a place as close as we could get to our mother's philosophical and spiritual self. I didn't know shit about how a person should say goodbye to a mother, but my sister's lists got us through. The minister spoke of my mother's contributions to the world, her work with children, her writing. Their voices unsteady, three friends, plump women in my mother's kind of pantsuits and glasses, rose and recalled moments and touchings that marked their memories of her. People chuckled when Mary Butler described my mother's embarrassment that her first published story appeared in <u>True Love</u> and not a literary magazine. "But she had a party anyway, spent the entire $25 check." I didn't remember that. I probably wasn't around.

At the reception in the church's parlors, gentle committee women poured wine (white, always my mother's choice) and passed little sandwiches. I recognized almost none of the people who patted my shoulder, took my hand. Even when I did, I could only nod at them. Smiling seemed weird.

What I mostly noticed was that my father had not shown up, not that I really expected him to.

A week later, Sharon and I pulled ourselves up from the bank and followed the rocky trail leading away from the slough. We took off what clothes we could and spread plastic bags across the seats of Sharon's new Subaru to sit on.

"Tell me Mom didn't choose the slough," Sharon said, as she turned the key and the motor churned in its solid Swedish way.

"Okay, she didn't, actually. She said somewhere peaceful and this was the most peaceful place I knew. I used to come here and smoke and fish when I needed to get away. I thought she'd like it."

"You've always wanted to get away, Sam." Sharon cleared her throat and sat a little straighter. "I have decided not to be angry with you anymore. I forgive you for messing up your career, your marriage, and your tacky lifestyle. From now on, you can live your life as you see fit. Mom wanted it that way."

"She told you that?"

"She said she hoped we'd learn to be friends."

"On her deathbed?" I felt terrible.

"Twenty years ago. I was fifteen and you were a brat. I wanted to kill you."

"Likewise. And, in the same spirit, I forgive you, too."

Sharon gave me her look. "For what?"

I knew better than to answer, so I asked her what else she had on her mind, since her eyes were filling up again.

It was the surprise that got to her, she said, that our mother would get sick and not tell her. She felt betrayed, as if it was her right, as first child and competent wife and mother, to be told about her own mother's sick pancreas. She could have fixed it. Sharon always felt she could fix things. I, on the other hand, knew that some things couldn't be fixed. And that a person didn't recover from disappointment or sadness or guilt in a moment of regret and a stir of brown water.

A few days after our slough visit, I went back to Mom's house. The rent was due in a week and everything had to be gone. Of the two of us, Sharon explained, I was the child to take on this job, because, one, besides being out of work, two, I had the muscles to nudge the furniture into a van and a storage unit. She would come by after the kids were in school.

A whiff of my mother flung itself at me when I opened the door. Lemon. Mom always made her Christmas presents, and a pile of perfumed yellow soaps, the leftovers from last year's project, towered in a ceramic bowl in the entry. She kept the defects for herself.

She had lived alone for fifteen years, except for occasional bouts of Sharon and me, the both of us finishing high school and going away to college and then returning off-and-on for a few years. When each of us hit twenty-one, Mom presented us with leave-taking gifts and we officially left. At least, Sharon did. My sister got a gift certificate to the best art supplier in town since she was majoring in graphic arts, and I, when the time came, not that I had actually graduated from college but I had made it to twenty-one at least, received a fat pack of typing paper and a thesaurus.

"Good luck, Sam," Mom said. "You have my genes." I didn't think she meant her hockey genes, but that's what I did for the next couple of years, here and there, breaking my arm once, my nose a couple of times, and leaving the thesaurus behind somewhere along with a career, a marriage, whatever else she had intended for me left behind, too. I ended up in the extra bedroom a few of times during those years, not my fault, usually.

My dad had already taken leave years before. At first, I thought he abandoned us because of my lack of table manners, but Mom told me I had nothing to do with it. He was an honorable man who had tried to love her, even though he suspected that she had hauled him into a life with her by getting pregnant. He never liked to make mistakes, though, and that had been a big one. When he found a woman he could actually love, no strings, he walked away.

At least that was how my mother explained it the morning the movers came and took his books and his leather Eames chair. She said he felt he had to save his life, what was left of it. She said she was looking forward to having her own life, too, once she found a chair of her own. At the time, I didn't believe her.

So that day I walked into her smell and a dining room wall room bristling with framed pictures. The slightly askew timeline of our family said it all: an Easter photo, Dad and Mom sitting on the old couch, us two kids at their feet, clutching our baskets, faint chocolate rims distorting our lips; our school pictures, gaping smiles, wet comb-trailed hair, serious zit-enhanced glares; the awkward altar kiss at Sharon's wedding; my arm squeezing Reba's waist at our new front door; fat-cheeked babies nosing into Sharon's breasts, her head bent over closed, milk-sedated eyes. Me, again, grinning gap-toothed, my own nose plastered and gleaming above my hockey stick; Sharon holding a plaque in front of aforementioned breasts, Best New Business; Enid and Will taking a bath together, Enid's' foot tickling Will's dick and he liking it.

If I were a poet, I'd say that Mom's entire life hung on that wall, and maybe two-thirds of mine. I blinked a couple times.

Then I went into the kitchen and opened the cupboards. I'd need boxes. I wandered towards the back of the house in search of some. The bedroom door at the end of the hall was ajar. Mom's room faced south and for a second, the sun slanting through the Venetian blinds made me think she was about to call my name, give me a hug. I touched a knob on the dresser, but I couldn't make myself pull the drawer open, stir up the imagined silky garments, poke into their secrets. Sharon would have to empty this room.

I slid open the door of the den. Books lined the walls, the bookcases, a gathering of old oak boxes left behind when a school closed, anchored to the studs after one of them swooned under the weight of its books and caught me red-handed and bruised as I was snooping through the desk next to it. That was a long time ago, and now an old computer hunkered on the desk in front of the window. Green north light seeped across the worn Persian rug and onto my feet. A small upholstered chair, maroon, shiny arms, nestled in one corner, a lamp perched at its shoulder. "Hi, Mom," I said. Her chair didn't answer, but the computer did. The Post-it note greeted me in bright orange highlighter ink. SAM, it said.

"She's leaving you her brain," Sharon suggested in her sisterly way when she dropped by that afternoon. "Maybe she thought you could use it." By then, she had worked herself into a snit at Mom for collecting all the stuff which she now had to get rid of, and some of the anger was sloughing off on me. "Migod, she has shoes from 1959!" I noticed Sharon hadn't switched to past tense yet and that she got louder with every cupboard she opened.

"Look!" Black puffy drips of the blueberry pie Mom had brought to New Years' dinner still curdled on the oven's floor. "That's it," she yelled. "I'm not doing this." I stayed out of her way as much as I could, opening and taping boxes, while she slammed cupboard doors a few more times.

We packed the books and computer, the part of Mom I was keeping, and Sharon set aside a small jewelry box with its string of wedding pearls and a ruby ring which we could not remember Mom ever wearing, a couple of cross-stitched pillows, and Grandma Lilly's punchbowl. We boxed the family pictures because neither of us had the wall to give over to them nor the heart to toss them, and then Sharon looked in the Yellow Pages under Estate Liquidation and called in a woman who bought the leftovers of others' lives. A day later, she offered us $5000 for our mother's. Sharon signed the contract in between a couple of sobs and a Thank God. Then we handed over the key to the woman who had already begun sorting through the kitchen junk drawer, and we left, I lugging the computer, its keyboard tucked under my arm, to Sharon's car. I'd have to come back for the books.

"What are you going to do with it?" Sharon asked as she backed out onto the street.

"I could sell it at the Mac store. It's not old. Maybe that's what Mom wanted." At Sharon's sudden intake of breath, I added, "She knew how broke I am."

The car jerked to a stop. "You're kidding." Sharon turned and glared. "You're not kidding! Sam Holsti, get out of this car!"

So I brought the iMac home. It wasn't that I didn't need a computer. Reba got the one we had shared, along with my car. And the house. Not this house, which could double as a garage, maybe a quarter of the size of the ranch we had owned the two years we were married, when I believed that having a wife and children and a lawn to mow would solve my problems. Luckily, I discovered the truth before we had kids, just dogs, and I left that house the same guy I went in, but knowing that I couldn't trust myself with someone else's life.

Reba had kicked me out after one-too-many missed dinners, a couple of mislaid nights, and in the end, a quarter acre of foot-long grass in the front yard. "You don't love me," she said, "that's obvious." She said a lot of other things, about my needing to grow up, to figure out who I was, to not expect someone else to pick up after me, my clothes, my life. She said I had to stop living in the past or I'd never have a future. My mother sounded a lot like Reba a year later when she kicked also me out of her house and sent me to the garage house. "It's time to come to grips with life," Mom had said, "throw off your gloves and take charge, mano a mano." If she had been aware of how that mano a mano almost brought me to my knees, she wouldn't have said it. She was telling me to get into the game, play, like she used to yell at me when I was twelve, a center on my hockey team. I didn't play hockey any more, except in uneasy dreams.

I bought the garage house. And Reba married a nice guy who mowed the lawn and gave her babies to go along with the dogs. A little splinter of her lodged in my heart, though, and it still stung whenever I thought about her and about hockey and about what could have been.

Like at this moment, so I changed the subject. Where to put the computer resting on my hip? I made a space with an elbow on one side of the table and set it down. The cord dangled in front of a receptacle, and I plugged it in and pushed a button under the monitor. After a minute or so, the desktop appeared, empty except for a couple of system icons and a folder titled, "Three to Get Ready."

It appeared that Mom had deleted everything, the little essays, the stories, the correspondence, the research, the budget, her New Year's Eve resolutions, one list after another, her life. Except for this one folder. Then she wrote my name on the yellow Post-it with the orange pen. When? As the ambulance siren screamed in her driveway? No, she'd given this some thought.

Damn! She was still being the same mother she used to be, advising me, warning me, trying to understand me, she getting teary-eyed and hoarse, me twitching my foot until I could leave. I glanced at my watch. I'd missed the first half of the Packers game, which my buddies were watching without me at Shaker's Sports Bar. I didn't need this right now. I moved the cursor to Quit, watched the screen darken, and headed out the door. Some things could wait and whatever Mom was up to was one of them.

CHAPTER TWO

The next day I got some good news. The Feds had extended unemployment benefits thirteen more weeks. It's not that I liked not working, it's just that I didn't like working for certain people, especially Lou Perkins, the manager of Silver Skates Arena, where I used to drive the Zamboni and take care of the maintenance of two sheets of ice. Most outsiders didn't understand what was involved in keeping an arena going, the plumbing, the intricacy of the layers of ice, the need to keep things cold and warm at the same time, the grossness of wiping up purple slurpies and plastified nachos from under the bleachers, the fusty smell of the hockey bags and meanness of the little girls' graffiti in the bathrooms. Not to mention the greediness of the owners who can't understand why they aren't making a profit and cut staff so much that some days I even had to sell pizza and take tickets at the front desk.

But I like ice. I like the feel of it under my skates, the pickup hockey games at midnight after everyone left, the flashbacks to the couple of years I played semi-pro: the hat-trick-pigpiles, sticks and shoulder pads banging at ears and facemasks, everyone yelling, "Sam, Sam, fuckin' good, Sam," me at the bottom of the heap. No pads, though, at those midnight skirmishes, just a lot of sacked beer, but the high was same. Five years ago, Reba, lying in bed waiting for me, couldn't understand it, any of it, when things were good, when it all went bad and it all fell apart.

Last year, my boss Lou, a guy whose only experience on ice was when someone got hurt and he had to waddle across it with the first aid bag, accused me of sabotaging the facility by not remembering to clean out the deepfry pan in the concessions corner and in fact, probably starting the fire that knocked out the nachos and hot dogs for two nights. "Two hundred dollars," he shouted. "I should charge you," and I challenged him to fire me. And he did. And I got unemployment but no midnight hockey after that.

Therefore the decor of my home: beer bottles and books. When I was a kid, I used to surge read: all fifty-five Louis L'Amours, a shelf of C.S, Lewis, every science fiction book I could find in the school library, each Stephen King as soon as it came out. If I liked a book, I would throw it on Mom's side of the bed and after she read it, we'd talk about it, even after Dad moved out and Sharon had gone off to college. Sometimes she left books like *Grapes of Wrath*, *The Sun Also Rises*, her favorites when she was young, on my bed and she'd get red-faced and silent when I let her know how lame I thought they were. That's probably why I did it. After I moved into this place, I just stacked up my books after I read them and every once in a while I took them to Goodwill. Except the ones I really liked. They were piled in grocery bags, waiting for me to take over to my mother's when I got around to it. Too late.

I was procrastinating. All I had to do was push the little button and click onto that folder and I'd find out what Mom had to say this time. I opened a beer and pulled up a chair. I tried to guess what it would be, this message. I hoped it was not another lecture. Even though she tried, she never did figure out that I was who I was and she couldn't talk me out of it. She told me once during a pretty good argument that she couldn't help it, that the words welled up in her and spilled out in a torrent of love. However, I noticed that she didn't overflow at my sister and I didn't think that was because she didn't love her.

I pushed and clicked.

LEAVETAKING

Susan lifts the wild purple sweetpeas out of the drinking glass and, catching the drips in her palm, stuffs them into the garbage sack. Then she notices the teapot still clutching its handful of salal. She pulls on the brittle branches, dry sharp leaves prickly under her fingers, and she sees that they have rooted during this month. A knot of tendrils clings to the pot, trying to tell her, perhaps, that the spriglets of green leaves above them are not ready for what's next. She thinks she should try to plant them anyway, as she stoops to gather up the dried berries that have fallen to the floor. Who's ever ready?

She places the bundle by the door to be dealt with later. Then she polishes the teapot and places it on the shelf where she found it four weeks before.

Now the kitchen looks just as it did the day she moved in, its oak cabinets and the old kitchen queen oiled and ready for the next tenant, the row of agates along the window sill the only difference.

She rubs her jaw, sore from clenching it the way she always does when she is working hard. She tries to smile at herself in the little oval mirror hanging over the sink and sees a grimace instead, framed in soft rays of wrinkles she hasn't noticed until lately.

The dog whimpers and places a heavy paw against her leg. When she speaks, her voice startles her. "Walk, Dino?"

He cocks an ear and his whine becomes a short yip.

When she opens the door, he hesitates, waiting for her to step out first, she imagines. "You still don't like it here, do you?" she says, pulling the sleeves of a sweater over her arms. "You think that when we go home again, everything will be the way it used to be, don't you?"

Dino lifts his nose and breathes into the cool ocean breeze.

"Okay, for the last time. We'll get the mail and we'll chase seagulls on the beach. One last time, friend."

The dog's toes click on the wooden boardwalk that links the house to the road. He looks back to make sure she is coming, and she pauses, too, to take in yet one more time the pleasure of the blue door, the weathered shingles, the magenta fireweed. She found the place last spring. Closed off from the road, only its door and a small stained glass window, which it wore like a jewel high in its eaves, penetrated the cabin's facade. Once inside, she was greeted by a tall arched window, a relic from an old country church, which filtered light from the west and framed the monolith that rose from the ocean floor a thousand feet away. Pines and alder shrouded the windows at the back wall. A healing green flowed into each room, drawing her eye and the soul into the forest's calm. The moment she stepped over the threshold she had known it was the right place.

"I have met someone," Mike had said. "I have never felt so close to another person. I want to be with her. Always."

For a moment, grotesque now in retrospect, Susan thought that her husband was trying to tell her that he still loved her.

Then she understood. His words slid about, sought a place to land, finally sinking into a gray painless tide and disappearing. She heard her voice popping brightly to the surface like a swimmer in a life ring.

"Bet she's out buying terrific lingerie right now." Her eyes met his, dropped to his crotch, caressed his ear, crinkled as her glance lingered at his eyelid. "I would be, if I were that lucky little lady."

Mike's chair scraped like a scream across the hardwood floor as he pushed away from the table and her.

"We can talk more about this in the morning," she decided as she leaned forward to blow out the candles flickering above their plates and the primavera that cooled on them.

Out of habit, they each rose, picked up the dishes and carried then to the kitchen. Moments later, leaning over the sink, rinsing away their last meal, she felt him leave the room. At the click of the front door latch, she folded to the floor, wet hands cradling her face, the dog pressing his warm muzzle against her neck.

Dino has been my only constant in all this, she thinks, as the two of them rattle down the gravel road towards the beach. Her sons had escaped into other worlds at their father's announcement. Within a week, Will had taken an evening waitperson job. Empty cereal bowls in the kitchen sink and an occasional scribbled note under a refrigerator magnet became the only evidence that he still lived with her. As soon as school was out, Jim hitchhiked to a Montana ranch determined to become a cowboy. And she herself had found refuge in this cabin, surrounded by ocean and wildflowers.

The day she moved in, she stored the owner's child's toys, the crib, the old rug meant to be played on, in the woodshed. She freed its windows of a winter's salt spray and scrubbed floors and black pots until the house became hers.

Then, ready for what she could not say, she poured a glass of wine and curled into the corner of the old maroon sofa and watched as the sun dropped behind the somber rock guarding the shore outside her window. When the light glancing off the ocean dimmed and cold white sparks flashed in the black sky, she went upstairs into the loft and went to bed and waited for the voices to speak, as they had done every night since Mike left.

"I'm sorry. I thought I put the blankets in this one.
"God, can't you ever do anything right? Is labeling a
moving box too complicated for you?"

The voices, their visions, chronicled the illness that had finally
destroyed their marriage, a subtle disease, she realized,
skipped heartbeats its only symptom.
The coffee table. He rubs furiously at a black ring which

matches the bottom ridge of the pot of ferns she had placed there weeks before. He sees her and throws the rubbing rag at her feet.
"Goddamn slob," he says.

Some nights, to still the dreary story unfolding under her eyelids each time she tried to force herself to think of the good times, but none came into view, not in that midnight work.

The dinner table. She is telling of her woman day. He listens, she thinks, until she sees that his eyes are narrowed on Will's hunched body.
"Sit up or leave the table."
Sounds of forks clicking against plates mark off the minutes until both sons ask to be excused.
"You were saying. . ."
I don't remember."

And so the exhumation continued, scenes re-enacted, each word repeated, each pain felt even more intensely in the remembering. And every morning, at her old typewriter, the ocean murmuring at her back, urging her on, she recorded her findings, fingertips pressing against the keys as if they were staunching wounds.

A sunny day, a dune, the grass flowing gently around their resting bodies, his hand touching her.
"No."
"Please."
"Not here. It's too. . ."
"Please."
"No. I'm. . .embarrassed. Someone. . ."
"Shit. " A cold breeze touches her breast where his hand had warmed her.
Later she had been ready for him but it was too late.

When she tried to rewrite this moment, tried to imagine the sand rubbing against her skin as the two of them moved in deep swoops, his eyes bright with pleasure, and when she was unable to, she understood she could have done no differently. That night her tears were as much for Mike as for herself.

In the weeks that followed, sleep came more easily. The voices dimmed and as she lay waiting for them, she sometimes imagined strong arms crossing behind her back, holding her tight against a softly breathing chest. Her dreams now bloomed with a sweet longing that lingered minutes after she awoke.

Then one night the voices did not come at all. The next morning, she found she had nothing more to write. She gathered the scattered pages beside of her typewriter and placed them on the table next to her coffee cup. She made plans to go home.

"Our last time down this road, Dino."

He looks at her and goes off to water his usual bush, to sniff at another. He comes back and nibbles at her hand, urging her to hurry. The gravel slips under the soles of her shoes and she needs to take her hands out of her pockets to keep her balance.

Dino stops, blocking her way. They have a choice--the short, steep cut through the salmon berry bushes or the riskless paved dogleg straight ahead.

She has always taken the safer way, the saner way. If she could just hold steady, she had told herself those first unreal weeks, not break down, he would recover from this craziness, this hormonal bleep, and they could get on with their lives. Not like before, of course. God knows I have my faults, too, she confessed to her friends. I accept my responsibility in all this, she had said.

She smiled when Mike came back to collect his belongings. "Of course, you'll need your Cusinart," she said. "And your leather chair."

A few days later, she called and asked him to drop by, to help her work out her monthly budget, invoking the Shalimar she dotted on her breasts, in the creases of her elbows, to lull him into staying longer, into remembering. He had entered the house wary-eyed and left in an hour, still unsmiling, looking scared, she thought. It would take time. She had time.

Then one evening he came to pick up Will and Jim to take them to dinner. As their sons walked towards the car, the woman, his woman, got out and reached for their hands. Their hands reached back, touched, they grinned at her, laughing at something she said. They climbed into the back seat of the sports car, their gangly teenage legs jackknifed under their chins. As they pulled away, Will turned and met his mother's gaze at the window. He waved. And she knew she had lost.

"This way, Dino," she calls. Together they scramble down the steep path to the road below.

"Scary, huh?" she asks. She dusts off her pants legs and crosses the street to the local cafe and the post office. She hesitates, tries to decide which first, a cup of coffee served with a cheerful "Righteous day" or checking on the possibility of a letter. Dino makes the choice, nosing his way to the Post Office.

She has a letter from Jim. A first. She walks to the bench at the edge of the sidewalk and sits down to read it.

"I think I will stay at the ranch. I feel good now that I can finally do most of the stuff I'm supposed to be doing instead of feeling like a klutz. Yesterday I rode a green-broke horse and today I helped shoe. I want to keep feeling like this for a while. If you write a letter to the school district, I can finish school here. Then I can decide what's next."

She stops reading to catch her breath. She has never considered Jim's not coming home at the end of summer. She tries to imagine a house with no children.

"Mom, I will come back if you want me to. Maybe you need your problem child around to get your mind off other things? I hope not. You know what I told you."

He'd told her, after walking into his parents' bedroom and learning why his father's side of the bed was unslept in, the comforter still up over the pillow, that she needed to get on with her life. This wasn't the end of the world, he counseled her. Weeks later, he followed his own advice and not looking back, headed down the road *to Montana. She, unlike her stoic son, had spent the whole summer looking back. Opposites, she thinks. Even in the way we grieve. She wonders what a green-broke horse is.*

"Let's call Will," she says to the dog. The town's one public telephone is across the street, next to the tavern, and she has used it once a week, a variation of a note on the fridge, to keep in contact. He's not having a good summer at the restaurant, not a good summer in any way, and she's relieved that the need to work himself into a non-feeling stupor appears to have worn off in the last few weeks. He is ready to worry about college, about himself.

She doesn't have change so she calls collect.

"Will you accept a call from Mrs. Thomas?" the operator asks.

"Who?"

"Your mother, Will," she interrupts and laughs and so does he. "It's too early, isn't it?"

"No sweat," he answers but his voice gurgles sleepily. "Are you okay?"

She hasn't thought about this for a few days and she isn't sure what will come out. "Yes. I think so." She hesitates, tries again. "No, not quite, but better." That is as good as she can do.

Will clears his throat and says, "Uh huh." He is trying to be helpful, she knows. She wonders what he is thinking.

Will wept when she told him that his father had left them. When he finally raised his head and wiped his hands on his shirt front, he asked if he was going to be weird.

"Weird?"

"Yeh, you know. How all divorced kids are weird? Am I going to be weird?"

She knew what he was doing and she joined him. "Will, you can't blame your weirdness on your father and me. It's all you. Sorry." She held out her arms to him and he fell into them, comforting her as she comforted him.

She hears him yawn and asks if he is getting enough sleep.

"I guess. I've decided that every other freshman will be just as

scared as I am, except the butts, who I won't care about anyway," he answers.

She decides he doesn't want advice and tells him she'll be home in a day or two. Then they can talk. He seems relieved as he says goodbye. Because she is coming home, she wonders, or because he wants to go back to bed? Probably both.

Dino has found a friend. He, even grayer than usual, rolls and rights himself, dust from his wiry hair rising like steam as a golden retriever scuttling crazily, toes spraying sand and rocks, rushes at him from the middle of the street. A man on the walk across from her raises his shoulders in resignation and smiles. A leash hangs from his hand and rattles against the ground as he approaches her.

"I borrowed him," he says. "I don't know much about dogs. I guess yelling at them doesn't help?"

Susan calls to Dino, but he's too far gone. "It's dog ecstasy," she answers. "They'll tire out or get run over." She smiles back, finally able to raise her gaze to his, an unexpected flush of shyness warming her neck and cheeks.

He frowns. "Shouldn't we. . .?"

"I was kidding." She steps into the dog game and grabs Dino's leather collar and shouts "No!" at him. Dino sits abruptly, panting. The retriever sits too, and grins as the man reattaches the leash and gives it a tug.

"You have to let them know who's alpha dog," Susan says, not feeling shy any longer. She likes the way the man's long tan legs move in on the dog's body until the dog is cradled between them.

"My friends didn't mention that, only what to feed him. I thought he'd be a good travel companion for the weekend." His hand reaches down to scratch the nose pressed against his leg. "He's been great, although a little too big to sneak in under my coat when I try to check into a motel."

Susan guesses he's about forty, a few years younger than she. The scratching hand has no ring on it. Only a slight roll rides above the waistband of his shorts as he leans down to pet the dog, and his shoulders have been lifting weights. Divorced, she thinks. With enough time to work out. Like Mike.

"It's a wonder you can even find a motel, this time of year," she answers. "Everything seems full around here, even the rental beach houses like the one I'm staying in." She tells herself she is letting him know all this for his own good, to send him on his way.

He looks up, not smiling, maybe shy himself. "Yeh, I know." He shortens his grip on the leash. "It's beautiful here, though. I thought we'd just walk on the beach for a while and then head inland." He turns toward the ocean which is green today, green like his eyes, and she wonders if they darken as the ocean does when the sun disappears.

The dead flowers are tossed out, the bags packed, the house cleaned. I'm ready to leave, she thinks, so what is this? She answers herself by saying, "We're taking a walk, too. Do you want company?"

The golden leaps up and nips Dino on the ear. Dino throws a paw over his attacker's neck and pushes him to the street, belly up. "Alpha dog again." she says. "Now that they have that settled, they'll get along fine." They move down the path, the dogs pulling them along to the sand, and as they pause to unhook leashes, she says, "I'm Susan."

He doesn't offer his hand, just meets her eyes and nods. "I'm Walt."

She slips off her sandals and follows the dogs to the water. In a moment Walt is at her side, shoes in hand, testing the water, shuddering with the shock of its cold. She leads the way, not worrying about talking, instead, out of habit, obsession perhaps, searching the beach for agates. She has found an agate each day she has walked this way. Thirty agates line the window sill in the cabin, talismans wished upon as she rubbed her thumbs against their cool contour and placed them in order on the worn wood. Always the same wish.

"They're good luck, you know," she says, seeing a translucent chip and picking it up. "Agates. Only you have to find your own."

They continue to walk, their feet now numb to the chill of the water, splashing at the edge of the ebbing waves, heads down like ruminating scholars.

She sees another agate, kicks it free with her toe and sends it bumping ahead of his next step but he doesn't notice.

"How do you know when it's an agate?" he asks.

She tells him to look for a rock that seems to hold the sun inside it.

The dogs fling themselves into the waves and the seagull they chase rises slowly off the water and floats over their heads. Undaunted, they race after another, drooling tongues giving them such goofy expressions that their adults laugh, and Susan reaches for Walt's hand, pulling back to only brush his sleeve, to point at a heron on the grassy horizon.

"Like you," Walt says.

"What?"

"You hold the sun inside you."

She believes she has imagined this. His green eyes tell her she has not. She doesn't answer except to call for Dino a few steps later, turning her back to the sea and away from this man, stealing the moment to taste the sweetness of his words.

When she speaks again, she tells him of the birds roosting on the ledges of the monolith and the secret beach reached only at low tide, hiding behind the rocky head lying in front of them.

"A perfect retreat," she says. And then she tells him of her own retreat from her other life to this place and he nods as he listens.

"A low tide in your life."

"Tide's seems to be coming in," she answers. "I go home tomorrow."

"So soon?"

"Yes. It's time," and she wonders if it's true.

Then it is his turn. He talks about his work, his travels, his music store in a small town across the mountains, a long-go wife, and Susan tries to listen but instead she mostly hears the beating of her heart and the joyous yapping of her dog.

After a while, they retrace their footsteps, the wind in their faces now, not trying to talk until they reach the path to the road.

"Would you like to see the view from my house?" she asks and he says yes as she knew he would.

They climb the road, the dogs trotting slowly ahead, leading the way to the cabin. A wisp of smoke feathers from the stone chimney and the arched window on the sea side glows orange in the setting sun as they approach. A wave of sadness washes over her and stops her at the edge of the road. "I miss you already," she thinks and when she feels his hand on her shoulder, she realizes she has said it aloud.

"I can understand. It's a wonderful little house," he says. "Very self-possessed, secretive. That grand window opens only to the sea, not to passersby. The stained glass is a come-on, an unexpected wink from a nun in a gray habit. Anyone standing right here would like to know more." His hand moves across her back and she knows he is looking at her, not the house, as she steps onto the walkway where the dogs are waiting for them.

Walt ties his dog to a porch railing and follows her into the rose-lit room, Dino running between them to his water dish. Susan goes to the sink and fills another bowl with water for the dog lying outside and Walt takes it out to him while she pours two glasses of wine. They settle on the sofa, she in her corner, he in the other, music filling in the space between them.

Later, when he returns with the wine bottle, he tries to sit on the cushion next to her, but his body perches awkwardly above hers, huddled as she is in the maroon embrace of broken springs that has been her haven for a month. They laugh and she scoots over and his hips nudge hers as he sidles in, caught, probably, in the crack between the pillows, his head inches away from hers as he raises his glass and looks at her over its rim. He wraps his arm along the back of the sofa, catching threads of her hair against the rough fabric.

They both understand what will happen, how they will kiss and stroke, behind ears, across smiles, how she will take his hand and pretend to touch a life line as she teases his palm and him into her bedroom, and how, in the green-black cave of trees and shadows, they will make love, cautiously, gently, exploring, remembering and then not remembering, fingertips anxious and foreign, lips murmuring love sounds, not names, even as they lay back moist and full and empty and want to, do, say thank you.

They doze and are awakened by the dog outside whose lonely howls become the music they say goodbye to. They dress and stand at the door. Susan rests her head for a moment on Walt's shoulder, his smell unfamiliar once again. He kisses her eyelids, asks a favor.

"The agate? May I have it? For good luck?"

She finds it deep in her pocket and places it in his palm. "My wish came true tonight," she says. "So it's yours to wish on from now on."

"Your one wish?"

"Yes." She can't think of how to say it so he will understand. "I wished to be returned to myself." She closes her eyes, unable, unwilling, to describe the warm slack waters she floats in. No tide pulling at her, urging her one way or another. No waves to fling herself against or into. No grains of sand sifting, escaping, between her toes, through her fingers. No movement except that of her own breath.

A cool caress breezes across her cheekbone. "Full of sun," he says, and she opens her eyes.

The yellow dog's paws clatter on the porch. Walt unties the leash and turns back to look at her as she stands in the blue door. He raises his arm, his hand passing slowly across his face, the agate, still caught between thumb and finger, reflecting light from the doorway.

A moment later she can no longer hear his feet brushing against the road's gravel.

When she closes the door, she sees the bundle of salal lying where she had left it, its roots dry and brown after a waterless day. She gathers it up, opens the woodstove's door and tosses it into the red glow, and the embers hiss as they eat into the papery leaves and erupt into tiny blue lights. Dino flops bonily to the wooden floor and watches as she kneels and pokes at the coals and then reaches for the papers on the table. She sits, cross-legged, the pile heavy in her lap, her fingers feeling indentations of the typed words. She considers the final act, the exorcism, the crumpled sheets flaring like dry leaves, the words she will choose to say goodbye to them. The flames are quiet, waiting.

The dog's sleeping eyelids flicker at the metallic sound of the stove door closing, but he doesn't wake up as Susan rises, settles herself into the corner of the sofa and stretches out an arm to turn off the lamp, the pages of her life slipping onto the floor, to be gathered up tomorrow.

My beer was gone. Two of them in fact, by the time I shut down the computer. Mom was not following the rules of our game. Sometimes she didn't. Like the time she blew a gasket when she saw the earring in my ear, not because of the piercing, but because I had borrowed one of her gold earrings. Or the time Mr. Edwards, my counselor, told her that the only class I was going to was auto body shop and she answered that I was in charge of whether I graduated or not; it was not her job. That did not fit our usual lecturing/foot twitching procedure, and I felt like a parentless child. A little like I felt right as I clicked off the computer.

I called Sharon and told her about the story. "It's pretty boring," I said, "about a woman. Nothing happens. She fucks some guy."

Sharon said she'd be right over to read it. "Sounds like a woman kind of thing. Why didn't Mom leave it for me?"

Jealousy, little pinpricks and sudden surges, were at the heart of our sibling malfunction. She had been the one no one worried about, unless it was about the trauma I was causing her by my teasing, hitting, and yelling. Teachers said things like, "You and your sister aren't much alike, are you?" after an initial enthusiasm at having me, her little brother, in their classes. She became a successful wife, mother, businesswoman and child bearer. She looked good, a little like Dad, with a kind of slick skin that made her seem competent and pulled together, a blonde knot at the back of her neck. I couldn't imagine that even as a kid she had ever had a doubt about herself, yet when she found a candy wrapper in my pocket or a new comic book tucked in the grocery bag, she'd whine, "Why did he get one and not me?" My reaction to her goodness was subversive and involved pain, a kick under the table, a punch in the back seat of the car. No, we had not been compatible, certainly not friends. We weren't when we grew up, either, only a little more civilized.

Sharon married a close clone of our father, anal in most of the details of living, including his monthly pedicure and foot massage and his highly geometric ties. Wilfred suited my sister to a tee, which was good for her, but hard on me whenever we all had to be in the same room together.

Half an hour after I called her, Sharon was wrinkling her nose at the day-old pizza on the coffee table. She accepted a beer and half a bag of Cheetos and sat down in front of the computer. When she finished the story, she turned to me with wide still eyes and said, "So there you have it. We're all there. It's a story of our family, the end of it."

"Except that you've become a teenager in a restaurant; according to your theory, the cowboy is me. There might be some truth here; Dad was a prick a lot of the time, I agree, but the lover is a figment, Sharon. This is fucking fiction. Mom was trying to be a writer. *Love Story,* remember?"

"We had a dog, Sam. Dino."

"So? Can't she use him in a story without turning it into a confessional?" The minute I said those words I thought of the magazine I found on the coffee table when I was maybe sixteen. I had paged through it, curious. This was not a literary magazine, even I could tell the difference, not that I was reading any of the ones that Mom subscribed to. For one thing, no authors' names appeared anywhere. For another, everyone was either kissing or crying in every story. One of those stories must have been Mom's. When she came home I had tossed the magazine in her lap. "What's with these broads, anyway, whining and giving out all the details of their love lives? You don't find men doing that." Mom just smiled. Years later, after Reba and I broke up, she lent me a couple of books, and I had time to rethink that thought. Roth, Updike. Richard Ford.

"And the beach house. The one we used to rent. . ."

"And Mom used to spend a few weeks at the beach every summer recovering from the school year. So?"

"So that's where she went the summer Dad left." Sharon stood up and brushed off the Cheetos crumbs. "This is way too sad. I can't think about this right now." She made her way through the beer bottle labyrinth. "By the way, the estate woman took everything except the bookcases which were screwed to the walls. We can unscrew them if you want to get them when you pick up the boxes of books. I'll be over at Mom's tomorrow for the final clean-up before we hand it over. Speak now or forever hold your peace."

"Or piece," I amended. We used to have little jokes like that, sexual jokes that we were sure neither of our parents understood. I don't know when we got so serious with each other. Maybe when Sharon learned her disgusted look, eyebrow raised, eyes rolled, the one she was giving me now. "Okay, I'll borrow Davie's van and come by and pick them up."

"You could probably live a week on the redemption fees from these bottles, Sammy. You might try that, too." Apparently my sister was stepping into Mom's shoes as my lecturer. But she had a point. I only had the van for a day--might as well put it to good use.

CHAPTER THREE

The peculiar thing was, I couldn't get that beach house out of my mind. Not only couldn't I imagine my mother as a one-night-stand, I couldn't imagine anyone else thinking of her as a one-night-stand. Her hair was short and gray, a little butchy like a lot of older women had taken to wearing it, and she had a round body that was not fat as much as packed. Once she asked me if she should have her bags removed or go to the Bahamas. I told her to wear sun glasses and go to the Bahamas, and she did. She laughed when her first grade students touched the freckles on her face and the wormy things under the skin of her hands and wondered how old was she, anyway? But I never thought of her as being old. And now I couldn't think of her as young.

I finished tossing the bottles and cans into plastic bags and started moving books to make room for the bookcases I'd left out in the driveway. I decided that I should sort my books alphabetically by authors, fiction and nonfiction, not because I'm that organized, but that's the way Mom's books would come out of their boxes. Mine and hers would merge in a way she would think was symbolic, and I kind of liked the idea, too.

After a few rocky years, we had ended up pretty good friends, despite her need to keep on being a mother. I didn't blame her for kicking me out that first time after Dad left. I'd been about as obnoxious as a kid could get, drinking, not going to classes, crazy wild on and off the ice, not caring about anything. Mom thought it was because of their divorce and tried to convince me that they both still loved me, that I wasn't the reason. I knew, though, I was just being me, looking for thrills, thinking I was free, finally, of my father's glares over the dinner table, and my mother out of it most of the time, talking on the phone with a friend or gone to bed early. That's about all I can remember of her from that time, tight lips, lights off. After a while, she let me come back home, and I made it through graduation and left for college. The next year or so, we communicated by checks, one way.

She'd like that I was blowing the dust off the books before I set them on the shelves. I had gotten to Fiction, T's, when I opened a box and found the pictures Sharon and I had packed. On top was the Easter picture. Mom wore a yellow dress, and she had a flower in her hair, which was long and wavy the color of her dark eyes. She was looking at my father, but her hand was on my shoulder, holding me still. Her red lips curved over white teeth, like she was about to say something funny. I didn't recognize her.

I set the picture on the T shelf, alongside a leathery *War and Peace*, and emptied the last two boxes. The room looked good. Homey. I found an old pair of Jockeys and dusted the trunk-table, raised cushions and swept a hand across the cracks and came up with gummy pretzels and thirty-five cents. Then I moved into the kitchen and wiped down the drainboards and refrigerator door and put a couple of crusted Wheaties bowls into the dishwasher. I was on some kind of mission but before I had figured out what, the phone rang and it was Sharon.

"Well?" she said, like I could long-distance mind read.

"What?"

"What else is on the computer?" When I didn't answer, she exhaled into my ear. "Migod, I can't believe you. Aren't you curious? Don't you want to know what Mom is trying to tell you?"

I needed to know something else. "Sharon, do you think Mom was beautiful, when she was young, I mean."

"Of course she was. She was beautiful at sixty. What are you talking about?"

"I don't know. I just can't seem to remember what she looked like."

"You were too busy driving her crazy to look at her."

"I can't imagine her having sex."
"You're not supposed to. She's your mother. What is this about?"
"I cleaned my house today. You'd be amazed."
"I'm coming over on my way to yoga."

CHAPTER FOUR

Sharon glanced at the computer as she took off her coat and tossed it on the sofa. Then she picked it up and said, "Sorry. I thought I was in your old house. Where should I hang this?"

"No, I haven't," I answered. "Not sure I'm going to. It's like undressing her."

Sharon fiddled with her coat and finally handed it to me and sat down. "Look. I've thought this through. You don't that it really happened, do you?" Glancing at me, she said, "You do! And you can't stand it!'

At the moment, what I couldn't stand was her sisterly condescension. "She could have, you know," I counterattacked. "She could have picked up some guy. Just because she didn't tell you all about it doesn't mean it didn't happen."

My sister did that thing with her lips which meant I don't know fuck and shook her head, "That part about the underwear." Her chin lowered, rested on her fist. "That's my scene. My and Wilfred's scene. A couple of years ago. I said it, yelled it, and Wilfred left."

"How--"

"I told Mom the next day. Wilfred came back a week later, tail between legs, so to speak, said he missed the kids. Mom told me to take him back. Kids needed two parents. 'Look at you guys,' she said, 'all screwed up.' So I did."

Sharon was the least screwed up person I knew. Her life had been so normal, so on schedule, except maybe the little blip she just confessed, that it could be a chapter in the text on how to be a successful adult. College, a couple of years as a free lance designer, then her own shop, marriage to an up-and-coming financial advisor, two kids who fought in the usual way and sang Julie Andrews songs after hearing them once. She was V.P. of the PTA, for godsakes. "Lingerie?" I asked.

"It was the only thing I could think of at the moment." Sharon was looking around the room again. "I can't believe it, Sam. I feel like I'm being hugged by Mom's books." She paused. "Omigod! They're alphabetized! Even I haven't gotten around to that!"

"So you and Wilfred are all right?" I was not sure what I would do if she said no. Everyone had to have something solid and predictable in his life, even if it was only his sister's marriage.

"Of course. Life goes on. Mom said that."

"To me it was, 'Get a life.' She was an excellent advice giver."

Sharon stood up and reached for the coat I was sitting on. "We have a coat rack in the basement; it'll be a house warming gift to you." She took another look around the room, reached up and pulled a book from the shelf. "May I? I always wanted to read Turgenev."

I figured I could sit out the next thirteen weeks of unemployment checks reading. I could re-read the books I had saved for that purpose but knew I never would. And I could read Mom's books as if she'd thrown them on my bed. With that thought, I pulled out a title from the A's, still feeling organized, but hunger led me into the kitchen before I opened it. I forgot I had cleaned out the fridge. A jar of jalapeno peppers and a chunk of jicama huddled inside, remains of an unsuccessful evening with a Hispanic woman. Jicama is not an aphrodisiac, at least in her case. Neither was beer.

When Reba and I were married, I used to bitch at her when there was no milk for my cereal or when she washed out the coffee pot with soap. At the time I hadn't thought of it as bitching, more like communicating my needs. Now, with no one to communicate my needs to, all I could say was, "Fuck, no beer," and then go out to get some. Which I did, taking along the sack of dirty clothes I'd been storing for three weeks behind the bedroom door. If I planned it right, I could make it to Sudsy Wash before I met my buds at Shaker's.

"You should separate them," a voice behind me advised.

"Look, these clothes are lucky to get this far," I answered. "They should be glad I had change for soap."

The girl moved in next to me. "Your underwear is gray."

"So?

"So you have to bleach 'em. We like them white." The silver ring in her nostril reflected the attitude in her voice. "Without holes."

She was a goth kid, black hair cut across the tips of her ears, straight bangs, eyes smoky at the edges, green in the center, and she was looking me over with them. "Bet you haven't had much luck lately. Try bleach."

She turned and walked over to the change machine. She looked good from behind, tight-jeaned ass, leather jacket. When she came back she held out a packet to me. "Bleach." Then she pulled a couple of skivvies out of my washing machine, along with some athletic socks and a jock strap, and she dumped them in the next machine. She must have taken my surprised silence for ignorance. "First soap, then the bleach," she said. "You can do it."

She plugged some coins into a couple of dryers down the line and concentrated on turning the knobs. Then she walked out. So I rescued a white T-shirt and four more sox from the first washer and did the soap/bleach thing in the other one, why not?, and settled in on one of the plastic garden chairs with Stephen King. The next time I looked up, my washers were finished and her dryers were empty. The laundry dominatrix had disappeared, leaving my white underwear flapping in her wake.

The incident inspired me to wash my clothes two or three times in the next couple of weeks, and finally the black haired girl came back with a laundry bag and a book. A beat-up John Irving. She glanced at me, and piled her things into a washer, whites and colored together.

"Hey!" I called over the machines' rumbling. "What about separating them? Let's do this right!"

She put her book on the seat next to me and opened her hand. Three quarters. "Separating is for the wealthy," she said. "A luxury."

She punched in the coins and came back. "These'll be drying for days in my bathroom." She found her place in *Garp.* I bet it said 25¢ on the inside cover.

We sat turning pages for a while. Then she said, "I don't like Stephen King."

And I answered, "I don't like John Irving." I was lying, of course, but what else could I say. Sorry?

"I don't like being scared," she said.

I asked why, and she gave me a slanted look that indicated she was wondering whether to continue in this vein. I smiled back to reassure her.

She went back to her book.

"I've got some extra quarters. Took back some bottles."

She shut her book, glanced at her washer which was as still as mine next to it. "If you are trying to buy me, you have. I can't stand clothes hanging in my face when I go to the toilet."

"Me, neither." I handed her a pile of coins and we moved our loads to the dryers. "What does buying you entail?"

"For three quarters, an hour at Starbucks." She was trying to sound tough, I thought, but her mouth twitched with the hint of a grin.

"Done." I took her arm and headed her out the door. "While the clothes dry."

Maybe it was the nose ring, but Rose was one of the few women I'd sat across a table from that I didn't immediately give a rating. Like: ten for hot, two for I'd rather eat snails. Instead, I just wondered about her. What had led her to the non-human black hair? What vision encouraged the insertion of ten earrings in her left ear? Her nails were black, scary. I looked at my own, and, under the table, started fishing out the gunk with an index fingernail. I stopped when I realized she was watching me. "So, besides laundry, what do you do?" she asked

For some reason, I think it was her steady jade eyes, it seemed important that I did something besides sit around reading my dead mother's books. "I'm working on a novel." I didn't say that I was reading one, not writing one.

Rose's eyebrows lifted. "Really! Yeh, I guess that fits." She settled back and raised her paper cup at me in a kind of salute. "I'm a writer, too. When I'm not trying to earn enough to run the dryer."

"So how do you do that?"

"Not important. Tell me about your novel."

I should have ended it right then and said I didn't like to talk about what I was in the middle of, but her teeth, a slight white overbite, were pressing on her bottom lip in an interested way. No one had looked at me like that since Reba. So I said, "It's about a guy with huge ambitions who falls for the wrong woman and finds himself in a motel room shooting up the night he is supposed to be signing off on a fifty-millon-dollar deal with his venture capital boss." A little Maugham, Tom Wolfe, thanks to my mother, and maybe a little Armistead Maupin.

"And?"

"I can't talk about the rest. Takes the energy out of the writing to explain too much."

"So you write every day? You don't have to work?" She corrected herself. "Do you do anything other than write?" Envy tinged her words, made her face go solemn.

Damn. A very deep hole. I tried climbing out. "My mom died. She left me enough money to do this for a while." Then I choked on my latte, and gave myself a few seconds for the half-truth to become whole. "And a computer."

Rose nodded. "Oh," she said.

I cleared my throat, wiped my nose on my napkin, and asked her what she did when she wasn't writing. She sold flowers. She went to the flower market every morning and arranged her finds into bouquets to sell at a booth outside at an upscale grocery store. Then she returned to her studio apartment and, surrounded by week-old ranunculus and oriental lilies, she typed on her second-hand Smith Corona word processor.

"Sometimes I go out with friends to hear music or drink coffee. Not at Starbucks. Never at Starbucks. My friends would gag if they saw me here right now."

"So why did you suggest it?

"Because you'd probably gag if you saw our coffee house."

This was going nowhere. I'm balding and she was . . ."How old are you?"

"Twenty-three. How about you?"

She didn't flinch when I told her. Thirty three. "My stories have been about old men and young women lately. Maybe you'd like to read one? Give me some feedback?" So that's how we set up our next meeting. A reading at my house. I was to let her know if she got the old guy right.

CHAPTER FIVE

An ambitious winner brought to his knees by lust for a wicked woman. One of the four plots in literature, my mother would have suggested. Macbeth. . . . But what if the guy was an ambitious loser, a normal kind of guy with one chance that he fucks up. Is that the end of the story? Or the middle? Even the beginning? This guy . . .

I opened a new file folder, titled it Jack. Jack was thirty-four, I decided. He had had fifteen jobs since he graduated from community college in welding or maybe aerodynamics. He was a skateboarder. In his spare time, he built boards. Damn. I clicked and got a blank document and looked out the window. I started typing. "Jack. . ."

The front door slammed.

"No! You're reading it without me, aren't you?" My sister swooped in, hovered over my shoulder like a hungry crow. "Jack?"

I hit the delete button.

"You should have called me. She was my mother, too, you know. Lucky I was driving by." She took off her jacket, hung it on the coat rack she still held in one hand, and pulled up a chair at my side. "Okay, let's see it."

Sharon folded her arms across her chest, a strand of her blonde hair straggling into the collar of her silk blouse in an uncharacteristic way. My sister's hair didn't straggle. Ever.

"What's wrong?"

"Nothing. I just think that you might want to let me in on this little incestuous relationship you and Mom are having."

"A little overstated, I think," I said. Even in our most siblingish moments she'd never suggested incest.

Sharon wasn't finished. "It's always been this way, hasn't it? I work my butt off being everything they ever wanted including a stupid May Queen that made me want to puke onto the Maypole, and you fuck off, disappear, drug out, run out of a marriage, and in the end, you get the computer."

"I didn't drug out. Just a little."

"And now that she's gone, I've got no one." Sharon moaned and wiped her nose with her wrist. "No one, Sammy."

Something told me not to remind her of her husband, wonderful Wilfred, or her children, the lights of her life. I waited until she hiccoughed to a stop and asked for a glass of wine. Beer would do. Thanks.

'I'm sorry, Sam. I'm wigging out. Things have been a little strange at home and I took it out on you. Did I always do that?"

I loved the possibility of saying "Yes," but I just shrugged. For once in my adult life, I was feeling a little sorry for her and I didn't know why. Her being jealous of me, maybe. Or maybe it was the little drip of snot hanging on the tip of her nose. "Okay, let's do it."

Jack would have to wait a while. We hunched in front of the computer and I tapped the mouse twice. Mom's next message from outer space appeared on the screen.

THE FIRST TIME

I met Adrien at a jazz concert in the middle of a meadow. When he asked if he could sit on the corner of my blanket since the grass was all taken up with bodies and mats and hampers, I obliged since I was feeling a little like a lost raft in the middle of an ocean of surging music and lolling people.

"Alone?" he commented and I nodded with a brave smile which I intended to mean that I liked it that way. Adrien mimicked it back to me and said, "Me, too," and I guess we both decided to test the waters.

During the break, he pulled a folded piece of paper out of his wallet and asked when my birthday was. December. He said I had to tell him the year, too, for him to be able to tell my Chinese fortune. I told him the truth and he told me that I was creative, kind, and about to enter a new life. I laughed and said that I knew that already. What else? He glanced up at me and added, "You are also good to look at."

At the end of the concert he wrote down my name and telephone number on a little tablet he carried in his pocket and promised he would call. Instead, a couple of weeks later he wrote a note and asked to be invited to the beach house where I would be spending some time with my dog Dino learning to be single again. How could I say no? No one had told me that I was good to look at for fifteen years. And I was feeling a little rafty again.

He came on a sunny Thursday morning while I sat at the kitchen table sending out messages to the world. An SOS to my attorney, a How Could You to my almost-ex, applications to jobs in foreign places. I was so busy trying to organize a new life for myself that I was startled when the dog barked and Adrien's head appeared in the door's oval window. I jumped and he smiled at me through his beard and glasses and came in. Dino the Dog leaped at his belt, the smell of what the man had brought.

"Some goodies for us. Stopped at my favorite deli on my way out." He set the paper bag on the table and began pulling packages out of it.

"Camembert, crackers, sausages, French bread, shiny red apples and. . ." He held up a wine bottle and peeled the price sticker off with his thumbnail. "A light Bordeaux, highly recommended for picnic-type spreads. And for you, . . ." He reached into the bag and took out three roses and a small glass vase. "From my garden." I was relieved that I finally had something to do. I filled the vase with water and poked the roses into it and said they were beautiful and I closed my eyes and sniffed the pink sweet scent.

We piled my papers on a chair and set the table and sat down and solemnly tasted the cheese. He opened the wine and poured us each a glass. For a while we didn't say anything, just chewed and smiled until he raised his glass and said, "We are celebrating my new job. I just heard today."

Then he told me about himself, how he was forty and taught grade school and lived for music and loved someone once. He parted his beard with his fingers as he talked, brushing away crumbs caught there.

I thought he was handsome. I imagined how I seemed to him: middle-aged, scared, ready? That was how I felt.

When we finished eating, Adrien brought in his tape deck and we listened to Dave Brubeck and Sarah Vaughn, slouched into each other in the bow of my old sofa like two shipwrecked castaways waiting for a signal on the horizon.

All through Ella I worried about how I would do.

He shifted to put in a new cassette. Dionne Warwick wondered why as Adrien dropped his arm around my shoulders and our free hands found each other. I tucked my head in under his beard and felt his Adam's apple vibrate with quiet humming. His fingers lingered at the edge of my breast.

I needed to make a decision. I had already made it. I touched his beard. "It's soft," I said.

I was surprised. My almost-ex's moustache was so bristly and stiff that it poked holes in my lip. One night he said he would shave it off if it bothered me--the way I had pulled away--and I said no and kissed him prickles and all.

That was part of the problem. I had never been very honest.

I was trying to change, though, and I thought I should tell Adrien how I was feeling. "Adrien, I believe I'm a little crazy right now."

His answer was to dip his head toward mine and kiss me on the lips, his pointed tongue darting about looking for an opening, and when I laughed, finding one. I pulled my legs up across his lap and got a better hold on him. He took off his glasses, laid them on the windowsill.

"And. . .?"

"I forget," I said and I felt a surge in my pelvis and knew my body still worked. We stretched out on the narrow couch, knee knobs bumping, arms wrapping under and over.

"And now I'm scared," I said, still working on being honest.

Adrien answered that he was too, a little. And with his warm mouth close to mine, he began. He gently pinched my nipples and licked my ear and kissed my eyelids and when I touched his lip, he sucked my finger and made soft murmuring sounds. His hands cupped my buttocks and he said I had a fine bum. I slipped my hand into his pants and told him his was hairy.

He laughed. And then he said, "Well, Meg?"

"Yes," I answered, and we pulled ourselves upright and I led him toward the bedroom, me bumping rudderless into a wall and wondering if he noticed. "I need to go in here," I said, and went into the bathroom to pull myself together. I washed and tried to look in the mirror, but all I could see was a blur of dark hair and shiny eyes. The elastic of my underpants snagged under my fingernail as I pulled them up. A hole gaped at my hip. I remembered telling my almost-ex that last screaming night that I bet his new lady was out buying sexy underwear for him. "I will, too," I yelled, "when my turn comes." Too late now.

When I opened the bedroom door, Adrien was already in bed, a sheet covering him. He smiled and it was a strange moment. Maybe I expected my first affair to begin with passion and ecstasy. Instead, I had a sweet man, under a sheet up to his chin, as if his mother had just tucked him in.

I undressed, turning my torn underwear and my saggy breasts away from his bright gaze. I was glad that I had shaved my legs that morning as I slipped under the sheet and felt the warmth of his body.

Adrien's tongue was talented. It worked its way from my earlobe to my thigh. For a while, I wondered what I was to do. Then I relaxed and swam in the flickflicks.

When I wanted to reciprocate, he gently pushed my head down, through the wiry fur on his chest. I bit at his waist, and lingered at his navel, and, like a diver seeking sunken treasure, plunged into unknown waters. Adrien whispered to be careful with my teeth, and I was, and when it was time, I lay beside him, my hands comforting myself and squeezing his nipple as he unrolled a condom onto himself and then he came into me, not patient anymore, and I raised myself in welcome.

Adrien stayed in me a long time. We smiled, touched each other's faces. I asked if he felt good. He answered by telling me I was grand, and his finger traced the track of a tear across my temple and into my hair.

"How are you?" he asked.

"Better," I answered and I slipped away from him with a kiss. "Thank you."

"Any time, " he replied and he rolled over towards me, his arm across my breasts, his breath moving across my eyebrows in sleepy waves.

Too late now, I thought.

A little later we showered, sneaking looks at each other at first and then soaping each other in a bashful sort of way, gliding hands along hips and shoulders like blessings. After we dressed we tried to decide what to do next. We sat at the table, picking at the cheese, and he looked at me in his quiet way and said, "Meg, I want to tell you. I've had a fine time."

I nodded.

"But I don't have deep feelings. Toward you, I mean. I need for you to know that." His blue eyes swam towards me behind misty lenses.

"I know. It's okay," I answered. "It's okay." And it was, really. I took his hand in mine and we went out to walk on the beach.

"Mom had a lover." Again it seemed that Sharon believed she should have been informed, but then she asked, "What would Dad say?"

"Our father has been married to someone else for fifteen years. What does he have to do with anything?"

"Because this was a long time ago." She tapped her fingernail on the last page on the screen. "Dad hasn't had a mustache for twenty years. She's just used a little poetic license, making it seem like she was single."

"This is not about her life, Sharon. When did Mom ever go to a jazz concert?" Not a good argument. For all we knew she spent every night at Jazz d' Opus, calling in on Sunday mornings from wherever. "And besides, she did the lingerie thing again, your thing I've been led to believe. "

"Maybe every woman yells that."

If Reba did, I hadn't been listening.

"And do figments always end up in the same beach cabin? On the same couch?"

"Mine do, only in a cabin in the mountains."

"I'm serious, Sam. This is for real. Mom is confessing."

"To serial couching?"

"She was human, you know. She had needs. Not like her son who has apparently lost all tendencies towards carnality, a case of beer satisfying whatever cravings he has. Have you given it up or something? You haven't been out with a woman in two years. Did your marriage tell you something about yourself that you are not about to share with your sister?"

She was kidding. At least, I hoped so, but a twitch of concern flickered across my synapses. I did have an experience years ago on a Boy Scout camping weekend which I still remember with a bit of churning. And I did lose any fervor I might have had for Reba's body during the last six months of her nagging at me. No, take that back. Not nagging. Trying to talk to me. And Rose . . not a bleep of that kind of interest. I blamed it on the nose ring.

Sharon wiped at a stray, almost-used tear. "I'm kidding. You're just on a sabbatical. You've been looking for pussy since you were twelve. Remember Shirley?"

The thing about having an older sister was that she had paid attention since I was born. She remembered, at inappropriate occasions, my need, at five, to keep my hand in my big boy pants. She had reminded me on more than several occasions of the time I cried because my campfire wouldn't light during my first cub scout excursion. At this moment, she was bringing up a girl I loved so much in the eighth grade that I poked holes into my thighs and inserted her name beneath my epidermis in black ball point ink. Fortunately, her name festered at about the time our love did, and I was cleaned up with antibiotics. I can still feel the scars of that relationship. Now that was funny. Why didn't Mom write about that?

"Okay. So Mom had a fling. Or flings. If you say so. It doesn't matter, does it? Anymore?" I suddenly needed for Sharon to leave, to let me get on with Jack.

However, Sharon was settling in on my couch instead, her hand flung over her eyes. "I know why she wrote this," she said.

I pushed the resting button in the iMac. This was going to take a while. I could tell by the way Sharon's feet were twitching, a family trait. "What?" I asked. I considered getting us both a beer.

"Do you have a beer?" Sharon murmured.

When I came out of the kitchen, she was sitting up, reaching for the bottle, not looking at me. "Mom's saying it's okay that I am fascinated with my Pilates teacher, a woman ten years younger than me and of very thin thighs, and who leads my class chuck-full of middle-aged matrons every Tuesday night at the Y."

"Pilates?" I had had a few impossible attractions involving athletes. Sally in sixth grade, who beat me at every sport, hockey, too, if they had let her on the team. The red-haired Harley rider at who played center in high school. The ex-Ice Follies skater of the muscled thighs, who taught lessons at the ice rink. Knowing, despite the hours I had spent sending out psychic messages and moonful looks to each one of these women, that I was of the wrong sex and not useful to them. Attractions don't necessarily follow the rules. Even for my perfect sister Sharon.

"You've got a crush." I said. "Enjoy it."

"Crush?' Sharon said. "I don't do crushes." But her voice quavered and she closed her eyes. "Well, maybe Senor Katz, my Spanish teacher. He admired my boobs, if not my imperfect verbs. And I admired the way he leaned over my desk, breathed breathmint on my homework. That relationship lasted until I flunked the final."

Another thing about Sharon, she could laugh at herself. I wished I could.

"Dear Sam," she sighed. I'll get over it. Except for the enjoyment part. You are a very perceptive person." She grinned and picked up her coat. "Got to go to exercise class," she said. "Don't worry, I'm okay. Human, but okay. Hasta la vista," she called as she closed the door, in memory of Senior Katz, perhaps. A moment later, the door opened and she stuck her head around it and added, "Mom's okay, too. Really."

Sharon's fragment of guilt was easily dissolved. A veiled word or two from a computer and all is forgiven. Again, I wished I was more like her. However, my mother's stories were sticking in my craw, joining the knot of stones I'd been carrying around like a toothless old chicken for a long time.

When I was a little kid and watched Mom kill and clean a chicken on my grandparents' farm, she explained that the rocks in its neck helped digest the stuff the chicken pecked at all day. My stones weren't going to help me digest what Mom was tossing at my feet. Far as I could see, they just weighed me down. I needed to stop thinking about Mom, about me, about chickens.

I went back to the computer, to the page I had started. "Jack. . ."

I thought about Jack and let my fingers do the walking. ". . . looked into the mirror above the sink, wondered if he should pluck his eyebrows. Hard to tell without his glasses. Actually, I look pretty good, he thought, the fake tan not too yellow, the teeth likewise. Ready for anything, he thought. Fuck the glasses."

Is this how it was done? Just let yourself slither in between words and people, let the scenes arrange themselves to accommodate your needs, to illuminate the dark places?

I kept typing, touching index fingers on raised dots, looking out into the yellow and orange leaves filling my window, wishing I could see beyond the white sky that would bring a winter of rain before I was ready for it.

CHAPTER SIX

I wasn't sure how to prepare for Rose. All I knew about her is that she drank coffee and listened to music at clubs I was reluctant to enter. So I decided to be suave in a kind of Fifties way. Frank Sinatra. Duke Ellington. Low lights and a pitcher of Manhattans. We'd sit across from each other in my bean bag chairs, or maybe on the couch, and crunch cheese and crackers as we read our stories to each other. I'd wear my shirt open at the neck, a splash of cologne if I could find it.

Damn. What was I thinking? I didn't even like this girl. And that's what she was, a girl. If Shirley in the eighth grade and I had gone all the way, Rose could be almost be my daughter. Maybe the evening with cold Hispanic woman had thrown this literary tete-a-tete all out of perspective. Think again, I ordered myself.

The pizza was warming in the oven when Rose knocked at the door. I had a beer in my hand, coke in the fridge if she didn't drink. My manuscript, such as it was at eight pages, hovered inside the computer blinking orange in its wait stance.

"Hey!" I said, as I flung the door open. A beautiful black-haired woman smiled back at me. Her green eyes slanted in a dark Asian way, her overbite moist and inviting, her pink lips moving, saying "Hi." Rose walked through the door. She dropped her long wool cloak to her elbows. A silky T-shirt slithered over her upper body, black pants billowed above black boots.

"Oh," she said, as I reached for her cape. "Let me put this somewhere." She spotted the coat rack and tossed her wrap in its direction. White paper sprouted from her handbag. Her story. Twenty pages at least. This woman was serious. About more than the manuscript, maybe. Where was the pitcher of Manhattans when I needed it? I led her to the sofa, not the bean bag in that outfit, remembered the bottle of white wine in the fridge, took the pizza out of the oven and cut it into a small puzzle of bites, hors d'oeuvres, sort of.

When I got back to her with the wine, I was relieved to see that she still had a piece of her generation in her nose. This time it was a small diamond. She looked at me, her eyes ocean cool. "Terrific books. I'm a little surprised." I was debating whether or not to explain them when she asked, "Who reads first? And we have to set some rules. No cruelty and no syncophanting. The truth, leavened with 'I really liked the part when. . .' Okay?"

I could do that. But first I had to let her know that I flunked five Engish classes between the ages of twelve and seventeen and passed the rest only because I liked to read. I didn't know the difference between a semicolon and a colonoscopy. So what I said about her stuff would be only about what I heard, no mechanics. She could do what she wanted with what I wrote, but I hoped it wouldn't be too depressing. I was beginning to like Jack.

Rose read first. Her story, the first chapter of her novel, was about being twenty, in a new town, a girl breaking away from nice but stolid parents, trying to find a different path. Her main character ended up in a club, dancing on the table, looking around at the faces cheering her on, not seeing anyone she could call a friend in the beery goofy eyes laughing at her, stepping off the edge of the table, falling into the arms of an older guy who took her home, didn't leave.

I was sure the periods were in all the right places. I said so. I also said, "I liked the part when your character understood that underneath all the cheers and hands waving at her, she was still alone."

"She was alone even afterwards, even though Billie Bo stayed on, became part of her life." Rose looked sad. I waited, but she didn't continue.

So I pushed the wait button and watched my story, what there was of it, appear. I cleared my throat, read.

JACK

Jack took off his glasses and slipped them into his pocket as he entered the restaurant, a bistro, whatever that meant, a Vietnamese bistro. His myopic eyes allowed him to see vague forms at a distance, and he spotted the red sweater she said she would be wearing. He imagined a smile, smiled back, walked to the candlelit table. He pulled out a chair, sat down, searchlighted through a gray nearsighted fog and realized that the woman across from him was his ex-wife, Vicki. She, not having seen him without glasses for five years, seemed to be having the same quake of recognition.

"Oh, my God!" she said. Her feet scraped on the carpet, could not get a grip, made her chair flail back, sending her into a backward swoon. "Jack!"

My characters got through dinner by frowning and squinting at each other. They finally managed to talk about the situation, "You wanted to be your own person, Vicki." Jack said. "I didn't know that meant a new name and hair color." His ex-wife answered, "When did you cut off your pony tail? iMatch.com should ask about past life, don't you think? Like former hair does?"

The story wasn't finished, of course, and it wasn't the novel Rose expected, since that didn't exist, but Rose said that she liked it, the melancholy, the subtle regrets. She curled into the corner of the sofa. "Keep going." she said. Silk flowers bloomed at her temple, framing her leafy eyes, the glitter at her nostril. I moved to the cushion next to her.

She unfolded herself, stood up, gathered the pages of her

manuscript, and glanced toward the coat tree. "I need to go. This was fun. Let's do it again."

As I wrapped the cape around her, I smelled rosemary. I walked her to the bottom of the steps.

"I live just a few blocks away. I'll find my way home."

I let her. What else could I do? She was in charge.

I picked up our wineglasses. How was it that Jack was getting back with his ex-wife and I, his author, was doing just the opposite, fantasizing about shiny black hair and green eyes. Not hard-core fantasizing, more like wistful thoughts.

Like, I wondered late the next afternoon, what if I walked down to the laundromat, would she be there with her quarters and her second-hand novel? Well, she wasn't. Only the Mexican lady cleaning up the place, who asked me if I had any business there, no clothes in sight.

Then I wondered as I meandered up town past the City Market, would she be waiting for me, her arms filled with tulips and lilies? No. Wrong season, only dahlias and chrysanthemums, in metal cans, a bored high school kid slumping on a stool. It was getting dark when I decided to walk around the four blocks of apartments leaning in on my house and met only three homeless persons and a grocery cart. The only place left to wonder about was a coffee shop tucked under an awning a block further on. Not Starbucks.

Coffee Tyme. A person couldn't walk by this place without falling over a golden retriever or a pair of combat boots. The heaters under the awnings made outdoor living an all-night, all-year reality for folks who liked to play chess, smoke, and, I was pretty sure from the looks of it, deal. I usually crossed the street when I had to walk by. That night, propelled by a sense of destiny and the fact that when I hunched over the computer a couple of hours earlier, looking for Jack, I had gone into a coma, I entered the heated atmosphere under the canvas. One or two people looked up; most didn't bother. I went to the counter, ordered a latte, thought that sounded too lame, told the barista to make it a double shot, and looked for a place to sit. Energy in the room pulsated in the same cadence as the hip hop on the music system, or maybe the lights were flickering. Whatever it was, I needed to sit down. I spotted a table.

"Game?" A person, yellow dreadlocks wagging like unkempt dog tails over his shoulders, stood over me, a box of chess pieces in his hand, a hand missing three fingers. He pointed with his pinky at the checkered top of my table. What the hell. It was obvious Rose wasn't here; I would have spotted the hair the minute I walked in. And I had to finish my $3.00 cup of coffee. I nodded, shoved my paper cup to one side of the board.

My competitor hummed the "Stars and Stripes Forever" as he contemplated his moves. He won my queen in four and I had trouble focusing on my remaining rooks. When someone yelled, "Hey, Malcolm, finally found someone dumb enough to play with you,?" I felt a little better. The game ended in a nervy twenty minutes and Malcolm brushed back a batch of wadded hair and said, "Again?"

Malcolm's sadism only added to the gloom I had felt all evening. I shook my head and escaped. A light unseasonal snow was drifting in, wetting the shoulders of the parkas and knit caps of the few people still gathered in the warmth of the awning. I had to step across a German shepherd wearing a wrinkled U of O sweatshirt. My first thought was how pathetic the scene was, everyone huddling in their coats over the dregs of espressos, looking around for someone to talk to, not wanting to go back to their studio apartments. But then, I didn't want to go back to my dump either. I glanced at my watch. I'd missed the Minnesota game at Shaker's. I turned up my collar, wished I had brought my knit cap, and started walking. I also wished I had asked Malcolm how he had lost his fingers.

One window was lit in Sharon's house, the kitchen. I went to the back door and called, "It's me," so she wouldn't be scared.

"You're drowned! For godsakes come in and get warm," she said, hustling me in out of the rain." Just like Mom. I even let her tussle my hair with a towel. Then I looked at her. She was wearing a faded workout suit and her hair stuck out in wads that reminded me of Malcolm's, except she could run her fingers through hers which she was doing right then, patting the piles into blonde straggles. Her eyes were puffy, red puddles. She looked terrible and I told her so.

"I feel terrible," she said. "I miss Mom so much right now." She ran a Kleenex under her eyes, closed them.

"I do, too," I said. The dart of pain in my throat told me I wasn't lying.

"No, I mean right this minute." She squeezed her eyelids shut then looked at me. "I want to call her."

"I feel bad right this minute, too." I pulled a beer out of the fridge and sat down at the kitchen table. "But not as bad as you, I guess." Her wine glass, ice cubes watery at the bottom, waited. She reached for the bottle, poured the cheap white wine she drank like Kool-Aid when she was upset. "So what's up?" I said, patting the chair next to me.

Sharon sat down and sighed. "I think Wilfred is seeing somebody again."

"Why?" I asked.

"He smells."

I was surprised. Not at the smell part. At the stupidity of a guy who fucks around and didn't take showers. God, even I had taken showers. "Smells?" I answered.

"Like lavender. Even his shorts."

"You sniff his underwear?'

"Damn you, Sammy. Don't laugh. That's why I don't tell you anything. You always make a joke as if none of this, love, marriage, dreams, counts. And, of course, they count. What's left, if you don't have any idea what you want in life?" She was mad, now, at me, and yelling softly, the kids asleep.

"Not much, I guess.

"You ought to know," she said.

My sister knew exactly where to stick the knife. It entered just below the unhealed scar named Reba. I finished my beer and pushed back from the table. Then Sharon was on my lap, crying into my neck, saying she was sorry. "I'm doing it again. Please don't listen to me." As she tightened her arms over my shoulders, I was reminded of another lap-huddling scene, one I'd walked in on years ago, my sister crying and my mother patting her back, saying "It's okay, it's okay." I remembered thinking that my mother never held me like that, like a baby.

I put my arms around her, patted her back, said, "Okay, okay." And I had never held anyone like that before. After a minute, Sharon sat up, bit her lip as if she was trying to decide something, then slid back to the chair next to mine.

"Thank you, Sammy. I know I might be paranoid. When Wilfred . . .when it happened before, I was so unhinged my doctor put me on Zoloft for six months. He thought I was suicidal and I probably was, but when Wilfred came back, so sad and regretful, I felt, for the first time in our marriage, useful. Strong, you know? Doing what I was meant to do. It was like getting an A+ because I had done extra credit as a wife."

I could understand that. Sharon always did extra credit. It was her way of life from second grade on.

"So?" I asked

"So, I can't do go through it again. I've used myself up." Her hands opened between us, empty.

"And what do you want me to do?"

Sharon swallowed. "I want you to find out who she is, where they go, what's so great about her fucking."

"Like a private eye." I still wasn't over the lap scene, needed to take a break, cool the tips of my ears.

"I'll pay you," my sister offered.

The idea had appeal. Since I hadn't been able to find a girl who lived within blocks of me, this second chance as a detective might help me gain a little confidence in myself before I, too, went compulsive and needed a pill. Besides, Sharon was asking me for help. Me. A first. "Okay," I said. I tried to sound professional. "Tell me what you know about the situation."

Sharon didn't laugh. Instead she poured another glass of wine, plopped three ice cubes in it, and told me about Wilfred's late working hours, the little coded A's in her husband's day book (which she had inspected in a closet with the help of a flashlight one sleepless night), the burning sensation in her stomach which always foretold disaster.

"An internal trouble barometer?"

"Yes," she answered. "I've always had one." She reminded me of the time she got so close to marrying Jerry, the basketball player, that she was ordering invitations in a printing shop when an intense bellyache told her that she couldn't marry anyone two feet taller than she was, shallow as that might seem in retrospect. "My stomach always knows, Sam. Reba's did too. Did you know that?"

I didn't need to know about Reba's stomach. "I just wanted to get her angry enough to kick me out, not sick." I moved on. "Wilfred, on the other hand, is being sneaky and cool. He doesn't want to be ejected. Something else is bothering him."

"Like what?"

"Losing his hair, maybe. For a lot of guys this is the first sign that life's not fair." I patted my spot of unfairness at the tip of my skull. "However, I prefer to live by Grandpa's motto: Grass doesn't grow on a race track."

My little joke earned me a finger. "I said, don't do that." She raised her glass, tilted it towards her mouth. "So, you think he's pulling a Dad on me, is that it? He's depressed that he can't get it up like he used to, upset about that wattle plumping up over his collar? Needs reassurance that he is still, what? Sexy? Even when he wasn't that sexy to start with?" Sharon had digressed, the two males apparently merging into an icon of middle age. "Did you know that Mom told me once that Dad was as fast as a blink?"

I felt a little sorry for my father. Women shouldn't make comparisons, especially when it involved a husband. Or a brother. Reba wouldn't say that about me, a blink. At least, I hoped not to my sister.

"Wilfred isn't. He's slow and careful. Shit!" Sharon' lips were hardly moving, her eyes closed, not in ecstasy, I thought, more in white wine. She managed to mumble, "I want the details. Are you going to help?"

She lay her chin in her upraised palms and closed her eyes. She was in no shape to make plans. I shuffled her to her bed, looked in on Enid and Will, and then settled on the sofa to watch Letterman. Wilfred wasn't due home from his convention until the next day. Someone had to be in charge here.

The next thing I knew I was being attacked by two guerilla fighters whose heinous laughs raised hairs on my arms as fists pounded on my chest and knees threatened to squash my nuts. I curled into a fetal position and pleaded, "Hey, guys, take it easy! I'm an old man."

"So what?" Will asked, straddling my hip.

Enid was kinder. She just licked my ear and giggled. "We're hungry," she said as she nibbled. "It's you or breakfast. Mom won't wake up."

I had a peculiar relationship with my niece and nephew. I was afraid of them. Sharon was such a perfect mother that most of the time I felt there was no way I could live up to my role as uncle. When I pretended to be a monster, I made Will cry. Once I tossed Enid over my shoulder in a spontaneous gesture of uncleship and she threw up. I brought gifts to birthday parties that disappeared almost as soon as the packages were opened. Finally, a couple of years ago, Sharon asked me to lay off the GI Joes and the Barbies. Maybe rainbow scarves and wooden puzzles next Christmas? After that, I just gave them checks and they gave me watercolor paintings of houses and dinosaurs. It had been a long time since I had both of them sitting on me.

"Okay. . . okay, I'll make breakfast."

My sister believed in healthy breakfasts. At least I figured that's why I didn't find Krispy Kritters or Captain Crunch cereal in the cupboard. The only liquid resembling milk was in a box. Rice Milk. "What do you kids eat?"

"Well, I'm allergic to milk products, so I can't have yogurt or cheese. I usually have oatmeal with brown sugar and rice milk, and I think we have bagels. I like them toasted, plain. Will can't eat wheat or soy, so he can have rice cakes and cheese and oatmeal with milk, but no sugar because it makes him hyper." Enid's articulation was amazing for a six-year-old.

Will interrupted. "I don't get hyper with sugar. How can I? I never have any." He reminded me of me.

"I have an idea," I said. "Where does your Mom keep her car keys?"

They pointed at the hooks next to the back door.

"We're going to try an experiment. Grab your coats."

"We're still in our pajamas," Enid objected, but Will went along with the program, pulling on a sweat shirt over his flannel pj's.

"Trust me, Enid. You'll like this."

We piled into the car, each of them clicking the belts and straps required of their ages, and headed out to the one place sure to please picky kids. Since we were mostly in pajamas, we went to the drive-up window, got our bag of Egg McMuffins and juice, with a couple of side orders of hash-browns. Back on the street, we headed for the park, the smell driving us crazy. We raced to the picnic table, opened the bags. Watching the kids dig in, gaping smiles biting into forbidden sandwiches, I was overcome with . . what? Not disappointment, this time more like loneliness. I blew my nose in my paper napkin. "Know any knock-knock jokes?" I asked, blinking.

"Knock, knock," Will said.

"Who's there?"

"Gnu."

"Gnu who?"

"Don't cry. It can't be that bad."

Will and I could be friends, I thought. Enid pursed her lips, looking a lot like her mother. "Stupid," she said. She would have to put up with us.

When we got back to their house, Sharon was sitting at the table, drinking a cup of coffee. "Well?" she asked, as if our last conversation had been put on hold instead of wiped out in a flood of pinot grigio.

"I'll get right on it."

We worked out the plan. I would borrow her car. I would also borrow her cell phone. She would call when Wilfred left the house. "Follow him wherever he goes and stake it out."

"For how long?" I'd seen those movies where the guy sits drinking coffee and listening to country western for two days straight.

"As long as it takes, Sammy." She called me Sammy when she wanted something, and it worked one more time.

"Roger that," I replied, saluting.

Wilfred was scheduled to return from his convention at noon. Until then, I had two hours to get my clothes washed. I did.

Rose didn't.

CHAPTER SEVEN

Sharon's call came at 2:23 p.m. Wilfred was heading to the mall to pick up some shaving cream and a file cabinet. He was sick of his desk looking like a recycling center. I trailed behind him, trying not to run into the Expedition between us. Forty-five minutes later he came back to his car pushing a dolly that held a box marked Hanging Files, Cabinet Not Assembled. He lifted the carton into his trunk, tied a rope to the lid to keep it down enough to see over, and drove off. I slid into a parking space a block or so away from the house and wrote down the details in my notebook. So far, the only surprise was that he shopped at Walmart.

Waiting, I had time to think about Jack's internet date with his wife. Would he come to the conclusion that a machine was better at judging the potential for love than the psyches of two angry, revengeful people? Would he try again with Vicki or would he could throw away five years they'd had together and start all over again with someone new? Or, I thought with an odd sense of relief, he could say fuck it and head to the board park under the bridge, his skate board under his arm.

The phone jangled. "He's going out again." My sister knew the meaning of cryptic. I started the car, rolled out, sidled along the street from which my brother-in-law's car was emerging. I followed him to a six-story building on the edge of town. He drove into the underground parking, and I pulled up at the curb a block down the street.

Lights were on all over the building, the Esquire Residential Hotel. According to Raymond Chandler, Mom's hero, I was supposed to watch as shades were pulled, and silhouettes moved behind them. However, the closed miniblinds at the hotel's windows weren't about to reveal silhouettes. So I probably should hurry in and watch as the elevator numbers go up, stop, come back down. Too late.

Only one scenario left. I sat down in the lobby behind a newspaper and waited, looking up at every ching of the elevator. I wished I had brought a book. I paged through the free counterculture paper three times, and at one point, found myself writing my own advertisement under Men seeking Women. "Urbane private eye, slightly bald, hockey nose, broke, bored stiff, can read, drools only when asleep." Not a pretty picture.

The elevator door opened. Wilfred leaned against the back wall, patting down a flight of hair over his ear. In front of him, a youngish man adjusted his tie as he glanced around, smiled in a vague way, looking back at Wilfred as they stepped out and the doors closed. They left the building, trail of lavender drifting behind them, the elevator continuing on to the basement parking area.

Wilfred? Damn.

I went to the desk. "A friend of mine is staying here," I said. "I think I have just missed him. Wilfred Knaus? Could I call his room?"

The clerk pecked at his computer, shook his head, said that no one by that name was registered at the residence.

"He must be here with a friend," I said. "Dark-haired young guy. Can't remember his name."

"Sorry. I wouldn't know."

I thought of reaching into my pocket, pulling out a sawbuck, slipping it across the counter and asking to see the registration book, but the computer screen and the dismissive look in the clerk's eyes reminded me that it wasn't l955 and ten bucks wasn't enough even if it had been.

Wilfred's car was in the driveway when I drove by the house twenty minutes later, and I could see the four of them sitting at the kitchen table. Wilfred's hands were raised, describing the size of something. The kids were laughing; Sharon was too.

But she wasn't laughing the next day when she called to tell me that her husband had withdrawn $l0,000 from their savings account without much of an explanation. "A loan," he said. "That's all I can say." He had kissed her on the cheek and said, "Don't worry about it." As he went out the door, he added, "I have a meeting tonight at 6:00. I'll be home a little late."

I didn't tell Sharon about the lavender-scented young man. Probably somewhere in the ethics section of the private eye association's statement of purpose it spoke of guessing as non-professional. And hurtful. Especially when your client was your sister.

Since my next assignment wasn't for awhile, I would write. I sprawled in front of the keyboard, waiting for Jack to decide what he'd do next, but after an hour it occurred to me that I didn't know Jack very well. Had Jack always taken the easiest way out, quitting when things got tough? Jobs, relationships, even boarding? If so, why wouldn't he quit now? I closed my eyes and Jack started showing up. His eyes were brown, like mine. Good enough body. Heavy eyebrows, curly longish hair, back at the temples. His wide smile made him one of the guys and attracted women. He knew it was mostly his fault his marriage to Vicki blew up. He had taken for granted her cooking, the sex, and his folded T-shirts lined up in the drawer. He wished he loved his father more. He wished he knew how to love, period, although he probably loved his mother. Who didn't?

I popped a beer and lay down on the sofa. Clearly, Jack was a loser. But he couldn't be totally without redeeming qualities, I reminded myself. You had to like something about a character, to care about what he did. He had a talent, skateboards, one his father never acknowledged. He had other feelings, too, like anger and loneliness. The beer helped. More of Jack came through. He was not only a skateboarder and a designer of boards, he also competed and was beginning to make a name for himself and a little money.

That was better; Jack was rounding out. I drained the can and opened my eyes. It was almost five. Jack would have to decide what to do next without me. I was on duty.

This time, I grabbed a Clive Cussler paperback and a bag of

Krispy Kremes, slid a pee bottle behind the seat, and settled a thermos of Starbucks coffee on the passenger side. I parked in the l0-minute zone in front of Wilfred's office, and at 5:55 p,m., he came out of the building and headed in the direction of the Esquire Hotel. I raced ahead of him and was waiting behind my book when he walked in. This time I watched as the elevator numbers ascended. They stopped at four and six.

I should have worn a hat or dark glasses instead of my usual NY Yankees baseball cap. The clerk was giving me glances, like he recognized me from somewhere. I waved, smiled, then I walked to the elevator and punched the fourth floor button. A moment later, the doors opened to a long corridor, arrows pointing right and left, no sign of activity except a maid and her cart at an open door. I walked towards her, looking, I hoped, confused. "I'm sorry, I've forgotten my room number, but my friend just came up ahead of me. Did you see which room he went into?"

"No see," she answered, yelling above the room's TV which her eyes scarcely left even as she threw the comforter over the bed.

"Un hombre?" I asked.

"No," she said, this time shaking her head and raising her hand. She looked as if she might be about to reach for the room phone, and I said gracias and left.

She watched until I got into the elevator. The scene at the sixth floor was very different. Canned electronic music floated above a small reception desk. A fifty-ish woman, her frizzy red hair held in check by four combs, peeked around a large bunch of dried flowers, mostly purple lavender, and smiled. Then I noticed the small brass sign on the desk. "Honeywell House."

Softly lit corridors led to both the left and right. A few of the doors along the way were open. The hall on the right ended in large windows, a sitting area, perhaps. As I glanced to the left, I spotted the sleeve of Wilfred's tweed sportscoat resting against the frame of one of the open doors. The air smelled of lavender.

"Yes, can I help you?"

"I'm sorry, I got off at the wrong floor." I leaped back onto the elevator and headed for the lobby where the clerk gave me the eye again. "Thanks," I grinned as I hurried past him and out the door. I looked up and saw that lights glowed behind all of the windows on the sixth floor. No silhouettes.

Back in the car, I poured myself a cup of coffee and opened the doughnut bag. No need to jump to conclusions, I told myself. But what else could a person jump to? Honeywell House? Soft music, closed doors. Bet that business wasn't in the yellow pages. Actually, I should check it out, I supposed. I punched 411 on the cell phone. The operator gave me a number. I dialed and the redhaired lady's raspy voice answered "Honeywell House," she said. "Can I help you?"

I hung up. So the place had a phone. It would have to, wouldn't it? A classy place like that. The only time I visited anything like it, I was led to a door by a girl in cutoffs and a see-through blouse from which a red bra was peeking through. That room had a dripping faucet and what felt like six rumpled sheets on the bed. The top one appeared to be clean, but I was nineteen and didn't really care. So this was how one did it when he was forty-three. Receptionist, even.

Well, hell, the place could be a massage clinic. Or a very feminine legitimate business, women's lingerie, maybe. Or a consulting firm with spiritually-minded clients. Like the young man I had seen coming out of the elevator.

I called Sharon. "See if you can find a company in the business section called Honeywell House." I heard her flipping through pages. Then, "Yes, it's here. Do you want the number?"

"No, I want to know what it says next, 'consultant' or something."

"It doesn't say anything next. It doesn't even give an address." She paused. "What? Tell me!" Enid was screeching, "I want to talk to him," and Sharon covered the phone and said something that sent my niece away in a snuffle. "Get over here," she said. "If Wilfred comes home, I'll say you're returning the car."

I finished the last of the doughnuts and started the motor. I wasn't ready to hand off any information. Not until I had figured it out. That was how P.I.'s operated. A solution in the last five pages of the book. However, when I got to her house, I found that Sharon thought differently. "I'm paying you, remember? Put your mouth where my money is." So I told her what I saw on the sixth floor of the Esquire Hotel. And in the elevator.

Rebanding her pony tail, my sister swung into her fix-it mode. "You have to pretend you are a client," she said. "Get dressed like someone from out of town. Go up and say you are new at it, you aren't sure how the business works, play dumb. Shouldn't be hard," she added, unable to resist even as her hand tightened on my wrist.

Enid flapped a box of Go Fish cards in front of my face, and Will pulled on my other arm to get me to look at his box turtle. My sister looked a little crazy as she let go of me and reached for her wineglass. I was conflicted about what to do next, was fending them off with a 'Wait, wait, everybody," when the door opened and Wilfred walked in, a bouquet of yellow mums in his hand. I nodded Hi and took the kids into the playroom to meet Cary Pace, the turtle, and play a round of cards before I left, minus the car.

Sharon waved to me from the kitchen window as she stuffed the flowers into a vase, her straight narrow mouth twitching above the yellow blossoms.

After three weeks of not hearing from Rose, I had been forced to drop by the laundromat with my sheets and towels every two days. On the third round, Rose pushed her way into the room with a bag so full she bent at the waist like an old crone. When she saw me, she dropped it and said, "Help me sort." Like we were friends.

She picked at the whites, I the coloreds, and when there was a question, like the sweater that looked as if it shouldn't touch any kind of water, we consulted. "What have you been doing instead of your laundry?" I asked.

She sighed and touched one of the purplish pouches under her eyes, not unattractive, exotic even, but unexpected. "I finished it." Her face glowed with the ethereal black pupils and dry lips of new mothers on TV shows. "I did," she said. "I finished my novel."

Neither silver ring nor diamond disrupted her smooth nose. A stripe of brown meandered down the part in her black hair. She looked a little like a grinning calico cat, white, orange, black, green eyes. I kissed her cheek. "Congratulations," I said. Her fingers dug into my ribs, made me smile.

After we stuffed our clothes into washers, we sat down and talked about finishing things. I confessed it was something I had yet to do, ever. How did it feel?

"Scary. I don't know what will happen next."

"Maybe someone should read it," I suggested.

"Someone has. A friend. He says he likes it. Especially the character I based on him."

Him? What the fuck? "Good," I grunted as I opened a frayed Sports Illustrated. Was I feeling left out of her novel? Or just as bad, out of her life? Either way, I needed to think this through, to remember that I didn't even really like her, did I? I mean, in that way. She was just a young kid, trying stuff out, finding her groove. Or maybe just changing grooves.

I glanced at her as her hand pushed a strand of brown and black hair in back of her ear, and I was relieved, for some reason, to see the earrings were still in place. Her fingernails were short, grungy, like she'd been digging in something.

"Him?" I asked.

"A writer friend. He writes erotic sci-fi and gothic novels. He puts one out every two months, self-publishes, and makes enough to live on. The amazing thing is that he writes them longhand because he lost three fingers in an accident." She held up a hand, the missing fingers tucked into her palm.

"Malcolm?"

"You know him? You met him at Coffee Tyme?"

"Friends?" So was this the guy she was getting over a few months ago? Malcolm, the self-satisfied dreadlocked chess geek? "He's a little old for you, isn't he?"

She patted my hand. "He's about your age." She stood up and looked into the washer in front of us. "Geez! I feel fifty pounds lighter getting this done."

"The clothes or the book?"

"Both. Do you want to hear about it--the book, that is? While these dry?"

She didn't wait for an answer, just plunged into the story where we'd left off that night we read stories to each other.

Her young woman, Elizabeth, abandons Billy Bo, meets a guy in a jazz club, a former clarinet player who had run through a glass door in a chemically enhanced fit and sliced off three fingers. Lawrence will never play clarinet again. When they first get together, they are both depressed, she by her isolation in the big city, he by the phantom pain in his missing fingers. She takes him in, goes along for his ride in drugs, and the two of them sink into a black hole that lasts for weeks. Then her mother calls, the mother whom she disdains for her cornbelt sensibility and miniscule peekhole on the world. Her mother needs to see her, tell her something important. She is arriving in three days.

They have to get the place cleaned up, themselves cleaned up, her job as a florist assistant revived, and one of them has to learn to cook. Or at least look as if they occasionally lit the stove. This part was pathetically funny, Rose said. When the mom arrives, she is exhausted. She hasn't traveled further than Chicago her whole life, and that was when Dad was alive and held her hand on the airplane. She doesn't notice the bong under the bed, or the baggies at the back of the fridge behind the broccoli. After she's asleep, Elizabeth creeps into the bedroom to recover the pipe, and sees four pill containers on the bed table. Her mother is ill.

That night Elizabeth doesn't let Lawrence smoke. Instead, they have a couple of late-night beers and she starts talking about her childhood: the playhouse her dad built that fell in on the dog, causing him to lose his tail and his trust in roofs; the birthday party at which her mom drove six little girls to Deep Throat having misread the film schedule; the seminal fight in which mother and daughter came to arm punching over who was driving who more crazy. Again, Rose commented, funny, but with a tinge of sadness. Elizabeth and Lawrence fall asleep on the couch. At breakfast, the mother informs them that she is dying. She apologizes in her quiet midwestern way. Her daughter wants to shake her, break open the sterile Kerr canning jar her mother has lived in for fifty years and that is now her coffin.

"Over the top?" Rose asked.

"Keep going," I answered.

The three of them go shopping, to jazz clubs, eat out, dance with transvestites, talk films and music with slacker friends, walk the streets, sit and reminisce over hot dogs on park benches. All of them, all opening up. The idea of death, both Elizabeth's mother's and, she discovers, her own, propels the two women through these days. Their last night together, Mom tries some medicinal marijuana, courtesy of Lawrence who reads a transcendent poem he has written that week. Mom confesses she had always wanted to be a chanteuse and she sings "Blue Moon" while Elizabeth and Lawrence hum the saxophone and bass accompaniment. Elizabeth cries, recovers, knows finally what love is. When her mother gets on the plane the next morning, each of them is ready to move on to whatever is next.

"What do you think?" Rose asked.

"What is it about mothers?"

"What?'

"They always have the last word."

Rose looked disappointed for a moment, and I tried to think of something better to say. Then she leaned over and kissed me, warm lips on mine.

"You got it, Sam. Thank you." She grinned and went to the dryers and began folding. Her mouth pursed like she was whistling a silent theme song, Blue Moon, maybe. She'd need a truck to get all that stuff home. Or me.

So that's how I found out where she lived. In a studio apartment that looked a little like my house did a while back, except not so many beer bottles. "I've been busy," she explained, as she stuffed her bag of clean wash in a closet and then started to pick up the dishes gathered on the floor around her desk. "How about you?"

I'd been busy, too, looking for her mostly, but I didn't tell her that. Instead, I probably broke a detective rule of confidentiality by describing my work for my sister, the mystery of the Honeywell House and Wilfred's visits there. "I can't get by the woman at the desk, by phone or in person. Whatever it is, Wilfred has apparently spent $10,000 or more there."

Rose frowned but didn't say anything. Maybe we were both thinking about the high cost of a midlife crisis. Maybe I should start saving?

"Writing?" she asked.

"Jack is still trying to find himself."

"No mothers in his life?" Rose got up, pulled a couple of beers from her fridge, and settled down on the couch next to me.

I didn't feel like dealing with lame Jack after hearing Rose's story. I also needed to explain my mother comment which, when I thought about it, had a lot more to do with me than Rose's character Elizabeth. "My mother died a few months ago. Did I ever tell you about her? Talk about having the last word." Then I told Rose about the stories Mom had left on her iMac for me, how Sharon and I had speculated about them and their meaning. Did she really have lovers? Or just beach fantasies? And what screwed up message was I supposed to be receiving from them, if any?

"Maybe it doesn't matter," Rose said, fingering my ear. "Maybe no message at all." She tucked her head against my shoulder and closed her eyes. "Not everything means something, Sam. Sometimes it just is. Sometimes stories just are."

Encouraged by her warm mouth so close to mine, I risked the question I'd been thinking about all evening. "So you and Malcolm weren't lovers?"

She sighed. "He is my reader. And mentor. And friend. I return the favors." Her eyes were still closed. "She wrote three stories?" She wasn't finished with my mother.

"I haven't looked at the last one. Afraid she'd reveal another secret. Like a fatal disease or something." I couldn't help adding that. I was still feeling a little jealous of Malcolm and, I had to admit, of Rose's finished book.

Rose opened her eyes and sat up. "You don't like the fatal disease idea, do you? What is it, too schmalzy for you? Just tell me straight, Sam, no innuendos." The lilac under her eyes deepened into an angry purple. Her pale lips waited.

"I'm sorry, Rose. I'm no good at this." I meant the critiquing, I thought, but underneath, I knew it was the whole thing, the head-on-shoulder thing, the depending thing. I was not to be depended on. It was good she was finding out early on.

CHAPTER EIGHT

When I left, Rose was curled up on her sofa, hugging her manuscript. I didn't even say, "See ya," or "I'll call you," which is unusual when a relationship is about to end. So maybe I shouldn't have been surprised a couple of days later when she appeared at my door and snickered at my white boxers-at-home attire.

"Wait a minute," I said, but she came in anyway. I pulled on my jeans and moved a few books so that she could sit down if she wanted to. "Coffee?" I poured us some very non-coffee-shop coffee, black with an oily sheen that sluiced as I handed it to her. Maybe I had heated it up too many times.

Rose smelled it before putting the cup down on the floor next to her. "I Googled it, at the internet cafe," she said. She pulled a sheet of paper out of her bag. "The Honeywell House. Look." She handed me a sheet of paper. I hadn't been on the internet since Reba and I shared a computer, but I knew a little about Google. A while back a buddy told me he had Googled all of his friends and I was the only one where nothing came up, an electronic non-person. He thought it was funny. I knew he just hadn't looked hard enough.

Rose had highlighted one paragraph, an excerpt from a magazine called, *The Best Revenge.* "Honeywell House. . . . exclusive treatment center for addictions and eating disorders. The clientele relax in designer suites, are served gourmet food, and experience intense individual and group counseling as they work towards recovery. A small number of patients choose the outpatient program which allows them to continue many of their daily activities. The professionals who run the center guarantee complete secrecy.

Clients are referred to the clinic by medical professionals or by friends who have gone through Honeywell House's stringent yet luxurious regimen. Cost of the one month out-patient program is $10,000. The client who stays at Honeywell House will pay twice that amount."

"Looks like your brother-in-law has a problem, not a lover."

Wilfred? That didn't make sense. Wilfred was addicted, if to anything, to organic vegetables and free-range chicken breasts. His body was his temple. He wouldn't put anything into it that would screw up any of his precious cells. He swore off chocolate ten years ago. He drank one glass of red wine a day, without sulfites. "Uh, uh." I shook my head. "No way."

"He's spent $10,000. No paraphernalia in sight. Maybe this guy has another kind of habit." Rose raised her eyebrows, peered into her coffee cup. "Maybe not drugs. . .maybe. . . sex?" She didn't wait for me to respond. "Okay if I get a glass of water?" She got up and walked past the iMac, glancing at the screen which had gone blank in my absence, the little orange light signaling its readiness to continue when I was. "Writing?" she asked.

"Thinking of giving Jack a fatal disease."

She flicked her green eyes at me. "It's been done." She didn't smile and neither did I. Instead, she said, "Let's read it. Your mom's third story, while we decide what to do about Wilfred."

I tried to figure out what to say. Maybe she thought Googling required a return favor. I appreciated that she was interested, of course, but I wasn't ready to share whatever my mother was up to with a person I barely knew. I probably shouldn't have even told her about Sharon's problem; I didn't like her guessing about Wilfred whom she knew only in her imagination. This was my family. Not hers.

Rose tucked a strand of hair behind an armored ear. "Well?"

"I can't, Rose." The orange light wavered, urged me on. "I need figure all this out on my own--Sharon, Wilfred, what my mom was trying to tell me."

Rose set down her glass of water on the desk. "Sure. Just

thought I could help." She'd gone blonde, I noticed as she opened the door and turned. Not a bad look. Sexy. "Let me know when you've figured it all out. I might still be around."

The door closed behind her. I glanced at the printout in my hand, but the words blurred. Apparently, I was feeling disappointed, like I had just let a hockey game slip between my skates and into the net. Maybe, I thought, some people are born to be on-going disappointments to themselves and others. Maybe our role in life is to make other people feel better about themselves, in comparison. And maybe us disappointed folks get off on the "poor you's" and pats on the back we get from our families and friends when we've done something stupid again. A guy could live a whole life on Poor You's.

By then I had a beer in one hand and the telephone in the other. I needed to complete my contract with Sharon and tell her about Honeywell House. From there on, it was going to be her problem. If she had a cokehead or a sex fiend for a husband, she'd just have to deal with it. I was out of it from this point on. I dialed.

"Who do you want?" Will demanded.

"Hey, guy, this is Sam. Is that anyway to talk? Try that again."

"Fuck you," he said and hung up.

I speed dialed.

"Yeh?" he yelled.

I tried to sound like a kind uncle. "What's wrong, buddy? You sound upset about something. Never heard you talk like that before."

"I am upset. The she-brat won't stop crying and Mom said I was in charge." Enid whinged behind his words.

"Where is your mother?"

"She's in her bedroom and won't come out. Enid won't eat her mac and cheese, and Daddy didn't come home last night. And I'm supposed to be at hockey practice." His voice had a familiar disappointed clog as he choked on the last two words.

"Hang on, I'll be there right away.

"Fuck you," my nephew said.

I jogged the three miles to Sharon's house and was gasping huge lungfuls of air by the time I got there, almost as bad as Enid who was being sat on by her brother. I separated them, wiped off both their faces with a warm washcloth, snot and all, and told them to straighten up and fly right. We'd head for the rink as soon as I had seen Sharon.

My sister had pulled the duvet over her head, her body a moldering lump. I glanced at her bed table, a musty wine glass, candle wax overflowing onto the wood, a rubber dome limp on the cover of a book. No pills. I lifted the edge of the thick bedcover. "Hey, Sharon, what's up?"

Erupting from her cave, she glared at me from between strands of hair that hung like yellow lichen over her face. "He didn't come home last night." She keened for a few seconds, like a sad old Arab woman on CNN. "I decided I would stop being so suspicious, that I had to show him I would fight for him, that I might even still love him. I got ready." She pulled on a sagging strap of the nightgown twisting like a red shroud over her breasts. "Honeymoon lingerie. Perfume. Makeup, for godsake. I waited until three in the morning."

"Hence the spent candles, the discarded diaphragm?" I guessed. My light tone fell flat, as usual.

"Fuck you," she said. It was not the moment to warn her that her nine-year-old son used the same words to express his frustration. Instead, I found another washcloth, wiped her face. I was getting good at doing that. I patted back her hair and told her that when she woke up, I'd be there with dinner and some news that might make her feel better. "Wine," she said, and I brought her the bottle and a clean glass.

"And," she added in some kind of detached afterthought, "he's taken another $5,000 from our account."

I hadn't been to the rink in a year, but I hadn't forgotten the smells of the place. Wet, musty as if algae might be colonizing under the rubber mats, oily popcorn, and the nostril-contracting sweet scent of sweat-cured pads and equipment bags. I took a deep breath and felt my legs tingle. Will's team was on the ice, so we got his skates on, my fingers shaking a little as I pulled on the skate hook, and then Enid and I went out into the lobby and bought a tray of nachos. The pimpled teenager serving them didn't smile when I asked him if he drove the Zamboni, too. "Lou Perkins still manage this place?" I wondered.

"Yep."

Actually, it looked as if no one managed it. At least when I worked there, I made sure the baskets were emptied and the floors wiped up. The glass window looking onto the ice was so fingerprinted I had to search for a clear spot to see what was going on. A pile of skates from the afternoon's public session threatened to avalanche off the counter and onto the head of the little kid standing under it. A sign, "Everything on Sale!" hung above the sales room door.

"What gives?"

The kid rubbed a finger over a zit on his cheek, shrugged. "I don't know. I heard they were closing the place. Nobody said for sure yet."

Enid tugged on my sleeve and pointed at the nacho cheese dripping onto my pants. We went back into the cold rink and watched Will and his teammates go through the drills, the same ones I had done twenty-five years earlier, forward cross-overs, side-stepping the blue line, stroking, full stride from one end of the ice to the other, arms pumping and driving legs. Blue line, red line, blue line until their faces glowed. Contact, breakout passes, the boards thumping. One kid in glasses, a yellow C sewed on his chest, skated so well his teammates slid all over themselves trying to catch him. Another's ankles bent until he was skating on the soles of his boots. Most of them, including Will, handled the sticks pretty well, shoving the puck from one end of the ice to the other, the goalies tensing and covering the crease with agitated body parts as the puck sailed toward the net.

Enid tugged at my sleeve again. "It's a girl," she said. "See? She took her helmet off." She was right. At least one of those padded junior huns was a pony-tailed female. That was the only difference that I could see between the nine-year-old me and these kids. "Girls can do whatever they want nowadays," I said, as I knew I should.

Enid settled back on the bench, quiet for a moment. "I want to be a fairy," she said. When the practice was over, the Zamboni came on and worked the ice as good I used to.

We stopped on the way home for take-out subs, to hell with allergies, and went back to their house. Sharon was awake, somewhat dressed, bending into the fridge. "We need to eat vegetables," she said as I reached over her shoulder for a beer. She seemed a little less unhinged, especially after she found the bag of broccoli, and by the time it was steamed, we were into our sandwiches and talking as if nothing had gone wrong that day. But it had. We all felt it. Will was sneaking looks at his mother over the edge of his onion bun. Enid's voice quivered on the verge of a wail every time she opened her mouth. Sharon's eyes were watery even when she laughed. I, myself, was having trouble finishing my beer.

My mother always said one should be as truthful as possible with children because they have sensors that go off like fire alarms when parents lie to them. She learned this the year she found a lump in her breast and our alarms turned us into candidates for the Bad Seed competition until she sat us down and told us what she was worried about and what she was going to do about it. We trusted her and we got back on track. Then, years later, our alarm systems having rusted out, she kept her cell count and her pancreas to herself, one of her few mistakes as a mother.

"Sharon, the kids need to know that you are worried about Wilfred."

My sister's head jerked up as if I had slapped her. "Worried?" She gave a little twist of a smile. "No. Everything's just fine. Really." She nodded at each of her children, whose eyes batted at her in disbelief.

Time for the uncle to get off the bench, get into the game. I pushed back my chair, looked at both kids. "Your mother's trying to keep you from worrying, but sometimes not knowing makes a kid worry even more." Sharon's foot nicked my shin. "Your daddy did not come home last night and that's what's worrying your mom. He has a problem, and he doesn't want to worry anyone but himself about it, but worry spreads, when we don't tell others what's bothering us. He's worried, your mother is worried, and now you are worried."

"Are you worried, Uncle Sam?"

Damn, that little wimpy girl knew how to get right to the heart of things. The question was, how to answer. I sipped my dead beer, put it down. The words skated out of me, singing over slick ice.

"I was, but then I thought about how brave and smart your daddy is, and how strong your mother is, I knew that the problem will be solved because your parents can handle tough problems. So I'm not worried anymore. I don't think you have to be either." Why did I feel as if this was the second time around for these words?

"You sound like Mother," Sharon said.

Oh. "Or God?" I tried to joke.

"Nope. Mom." Sharon leaned over and kissed my cheek. "Thanks. We needed that. And you and I have to talk, right? You've found out something?"

As I said, "Maybe," the door opened and Wilfred walked in, rumpled and whiskery, like he had slept in his clothes. The kids climbed all over him, and Sharon got up and stuck more broccoli in the microwave. I wanted someone to yell, "Where the hell have you been?" but no one did. My sister looked at me, shook her head, mouthed Tomorrow Morning at me, and I left.

The thing was, I was started down a trail of truth, but I didn't know where it would end. If I told Sharon what I'd found out about Honeywell House, she'd jump to the same conclusion I had, that Wilfred was addicted to something. Like Rose, Sharon would probably guess it was sex, since she seemed to have it on her mind. I found that highly unlikely, but you never can tell about these tight-assed guys. I still suspected drugs, probably high class goods, not stuff bought in alleys. Pills, maybe. But we'd both just be guessing.

I wished I liked him. When someone is acting weird, a friend can sit down with him over a beer and ask, "What's up, pal?" and maybe lend a hand without intruding too much. Davie did that for me once. When everything changed and Reba left, I was flapping, untethered, in the wind. One night after a midnight game at the arena, a couple of us went to every tavern and bar on 23rd Street. Ten, maybe, and the last one was the The Olde Mill. Outside this place a huge wheel pretended to grind corn or something, as it rolled around and around through a pool of water.

I got the idea that it would be totally pissant to ride the wheel all the way around, over the top, through the water, then upright again, like a baptism, a cleansing of my befogged brain and life. So I jumped into the pool, grabbed a crossbar, felt myself being lifted fifteen feet into the air. I hooked my toes into the wheel's skeleton, ready to go into the water headfirst on the descent. Except that at that very moment I felt the skin on the back of my hands being filleted off their underlying bones. If the rest of me had managed to slide through the passage between frame and wheel, I would have ended up three-eighths of an inch thick. Fortunately, I could still open my fingers, slip backwards off the wheel and into the water, which was pink by the time I knew I needed help.

Davie took me to his apartment, rubbed my wounds with whiskey, wrapped me up. At some point, I was able to say a whole sentence. "Not too smart, huh?"

Davie shrugged. "What's up, Sam?" It was probably pain or the sight of the blood still leaking through the T-shirt bandages, but I suddenly felt so sad that all I could do was choke up and hide my face under my padded hands. I was ten again, squeezing my eyes so tight my eyeballs burned. Davie patted me on the shoulder and got up and made coffee while I swallowed and blew my nose, and when we finally talked, it was about that day's football game. Davie's question didn't cure me, but at least my suicidal tendencies quieted down and I could go on as if I were almost normal.

So, maybe I should ask "What's up?" of a man who wasn't my friend, but who was loved by my sister, for whatever reason. I didn't suppose he would choke up, but maybe he needed someone to tell his side of the story to. I dialed their number and Wilfred answered.

"I want to see you, tomorrow, early," I whispered into the phone, in case Sharon was in the room. Wilfred breathed a couple of times. Finally he asked why.

"I think I know your secret. I don't want to be the one to tell Sharon, or at least I'd like to get the story right."

Again a pause, then, in a normal voice that meant she was somewhere else, he said, "I told Sharon I had been feeling ill at work and apparently went into some sort of fugue last night. Flu probably. I stopped by the ER this morning, but after a few tests, they referred me to my doctor. I said I didn't want to worry her, so I didn't call, not realizing that I had lost an entire night somewhere." He thought for a minute. "I'll tell her I have an early appointment for an MRI. Harry's Cafe at 8:30?"

Lying was apparently one of Wilfred's many talents. "Okay." I said. Fugue? I went to my desk. According to my mother's dictionary, it had something to do with music, unless you went to the second meaning: a state of consciousness in which one conducts his life normally, but afterwards can't remember anything. A fugue would be handy, at times, like when you've done something stupid or hurtful. Didn't happen because I can't remember it. Or it wasn't really me doing that stuff, just some out-of-control nodule in my medulla oblongata. I ran my fingers over the scars on the back of my hands. Unfortunately, I was not subject to fugues. I remembered every dumb thing I'd ever done. I read somewhere once that we remember the bad things in our pasts because when they happen, we are flooded with hot emotion, and the scenes are imprinted in our memory like brands. The good times, calm and cool, float through our consciousness leaving only faint tracks.

I sat down at my computer, but Jack refused to make an appearance. I didn't feel like going to Shaker's, although I did give a thought to wandering by Coffee Tyme. If nothing else, maybe Malcolm wanted to be entertained. No. If I was going to be depressed, I decided, I would be depressed alone. I picked up the A book I'd left on the coffee table. Even though the idea of spirits and mystic beings seemed to fit my mood, I couldn't make it beyond Allende's first sentence, so I went to bed. Maybe, instead, I would follow a few of those cool faint distant tracks back into my childhood.

I moved cautiously, one thought in the foot print of the one ahead of it like a band of Mohawks heading out, looking for game. At first I could only bring up times I cried or yelled, or someone cried or yelled at me. A fight that left me and my jacket bloody, Mom crying as she swooped on her bike around the neighborhood looking for my assailants. I remembered a few slaps, a whupping with a ruler, a week in my bedroom. Pieces of faces: my father's rigid lips, his eyebrows so low that they touched his glasses, his sign of disapproval; my mother's wet eyes glancing from one of us to the other, not on my side, not, I hoped, on his, a piece of flotsam caught in between two clashing currents, battered, swimming against one, then the other.

Then I came upon the night she entered my room, late, when I should have been asleep, the bed rattling as she settled down on it, her coffee breath on my cheek as she leaned over to kiss me. "I'm sorry, Sam. I love you so much." I held my breath until her hand pulled the blanket to my chin. She rose and closed the door without a sound.

What kind of moment was that, good or bad? My mother had seemed so sad. But I could still feel that midnight kiss, the feather of her lips, the warmth that surged through me. At other times, when my father said, "Good job, Sam," as he unloosened my skates, I had felt that sort of connection again. I felt it even now, years later, remembering sitting in the back seat of the car, a new toy in my lap, my mother's voice consoling me, telling me that everyone had second thoughts; there was always a next time to choose.

I heard laughter. The time my sister curled my hair in her spongy rollers and presented me to Grandma Lilly who asked, "Is there something you want to tell us?" And the Christmas we all dressed in costumes and Sharon and I were Mary and Joseph and our dog Dino was Jesus. The wise men, Mom and Dad and Grandma in terrycloth bathrobes, carried gifts of holiday fudge. The joy of those moments, and others, dangled like Christmas lights along the way as I stepped into the dark reaches of those years: catching my first steelhead, my first hat trick, my first hesitating thumb-brushing of a girl's nipple.

Even the disappointing times, the games that ended in defeat, the presents I didn't get, the fish that got away, the girls who called me gross, lighted this nocturnal path, informed my steps. I continued, a hunter following tracks, until I fell asleep.

CHAPTER NINE

Wilfred sat down across from me in the booth. "Well?" He looked a little better than the night before, but if he told Sharon he was going for an MRI, I bet she believed him, his eyelids still swollen and at half mast.

The waitress brought us coffee and I leaned toward my brother-in-law, looked him in the eye, and said, "What's up, Wilfred?"

He reached for a packet of sweetener, dumped its contents into his cup and stirred. "You indicated you had something to say to me. Why don't you do that?"

I guessed "What's up?" worked only between friends. So I told him that I knew he was going to a treatment clinic regularly, that for the sake of his family, he should come clean, especially since he had wiped out the savings account to pay for it and was making his wife crazy with worry.

"That's it?" Wilfred's shoulders dropped to their normal right angle and I knew I didn't have all the story. He was relieved about something. He stood up, pulled on his overcoat. "I don't think this has very much to do with you."

I threw a couple of bucks on the table and followed him out the door. "It kind of **is** my business," I said, grabbing at his sleeve. "Your wife asked me to find out who you were fucking. I'm going to tell her nobody that I could discover. But I'm also going to tell her about Honeywell House, about what kinds of folks are treated there. Sharon will ride that information to the moon, especially since you've apparently taken to not coming home. She will guess that you're back at it, whatever it is, and now that another $5,000 is gone, you're about to spend whatever it takes to keep it going—no matter how you explain away your absence with fugues and MRI's." By now I was yelling. "Of course, it's my business. This is my sister I'm watching fall apart, you asshole."

He straight-armed me into a traffic sign and turned away "Give me a couple of days," he called over his shoulder. "I might not be home tonight. In a day or so, I'll explain everything." He stopped, looked back. "I need your help." Then he did a very non-Wilfred thing. "Please," he said. He hurried down the street, around a corner, while I stood and tried to think what to do.

The ice rink squatted a few blocks away behind the dark boxes of a once-hopeful mall. I wandered towards it, thinking that I needed a little time, too. When I was a kid, I felt totally myself only when my skates were singing over new ice, my legs and arms working hard, my eyes stinging with the cold, my head clear and fearless. It would be nice to feel like that again. I pushed through the front door and saw the Zamboni driver standing behind the skate counter. I asked for size ten, hockey, and half of the sheet. The other half was being rented, I could see through the hazy window, by two middle-aged ladies in little skirts and leg warmers doing figures and cautious inside and outside edges. The driver took in my grimy jeans and asked if didn't I want to wait for public session, it would cost a lot less, and I said no, I needed to get on right then.

The ice was not quite singing, was more of a swish, since the Zamboni hadn't been over it for a while, but it still sounded good. I started with a few minutes of forward crossovers, then began to stroke around the boards, working up to a full stride, arms pushing the rest of me along. I breathed chest-bursting gasps, felt my ribs open, sink, stretch. Finally, I swooshed to my famous hockey stop and put a skate up on the board to stretch my hamstrings. After a moment, I realized that the two women huddled in the middle of the rink were watching me, perhaps fearful for their safety. I waved at them and yelled, "Great day, huh?" They waved mittened hands back. When the hour was up, we left the rink panting and grinning at each other As we unlaced and flexed our toes, the Zamboni came through the doors and we cheered. That guy knew his business.

We introduced ourselves. The dark-haired woman was Mary, the gray-blonde, Jane. "We come three times a week," Mary said. She looked at her friend, who nodded. "We'd love to share the ice with someone. Would you like to join us?" I noticed that the leather jacket she was sticking her arms into had a mink collar. Their skates were Klingbiels, hand made, top of the line. Next time I'd bring my Bauers.

'Sure," I answered. It wasn't like I had anyone else to skate with, and it was exercise, I told myself.

"Friday, l0:00 a.m.?"

Sounded good to me. I watched as they walked out to the Mercedes parked in the handicapped space.

"So you're closing up?" I asked the kid at the popcorn machine as I returned my skates. Norman, his badge said.

"Ask him," Norman answered, nodding a netted head toward a window, behind which a man sat with a hand on his forehead as he talked on the phone. "He's the manager." Lou Perkins, my old boss, greasy-haired as always, was shouting like he used to at me. He hung up when I walked in. He didn't recognize me, probably because I had lost my mullet and my nose wasn't plastered.

I helped him out. "Sam . . ."

"Oh, yeh!" Pieces of our last ruptured scene apparently fell into place and he frowned. "So what are you doing now?" He flipped the papers on his desk to let me know he was so busy he couldn't talk very long. A faint odor wafted toward me. Jack Daniels, I guessed.

"I hear this place is closing."

"I wouldn't say that. We're in negotiations with a buyer. Actually, an investment group. No definite decision at this point."

"So, what's the timeline for closing?"

"A couple of months, maybe. Sometime after hockey season. We're probably talking summer."

"We?"

"Well, Lee Chin, of course. But I'm the one who runs the facility, so I'm doing most of the talking.

Lee Chin, the owner of the rink, bought in when hockey was really big around here. Then Parkdale lost its professional team and he was left holding a leaking bag of ice. Lou was his manager. Neither one of them knew shit about arenas. "Who's the buyer?"

"Not supposed to say." The phone rang and he answered it. Apparently the arena office staff was down to Norman, Zamboni Guy and Bourbon Breath. I waved goodbye and shuffled through the candy wrappers to the front door.

The Silver Skates Arena had been my second home when I was a kid, and my first home the winter I didn't have one. Fifteen years later the paint was peeling, the windows gray with crud. The place wasn't saving many lives now, just two old women doing figure 8's in the middle of the morning when the ice should be filled with young mothers taking a break, their kids out on the second sheet in pre-school classes. I pushed through the banged up door, and stopped at the cross street leading to my house.

Not only young mothers, I thought. Secretaries and bookkeepers coming in at lunchtime for workouts that left them ready for the rest of the day, homeschoolers taking lessons at 2:00, followed by hockey and figure classes after regular school hours. And the old guys like me late at night, like it used to be. The arena could buy a franchise and bring semi-pro games to the fans, a show or two a year with guest stars. And all of these folks would line up to buy healthy and expensive snacks from a kid who has had his skin and his manners dealt with. I didn't care that I was talking to myself out loud. I had it all worked out in the time it took me to walk home.

"Yeh! And a November frozen turkey curling contest." I said as I opened my front door and stepped in. A pile of envelopes crackled under my feet. Even before I picked them up, I knew what they contained: a notice of imminent termination of electric service; a note from the IRS; a telephone cut-off warning. The message light on that phone was flashing and I hesitated before I picked up, heard Sharon telling me I could never be depended on, why had she tried, that I had promised to come and tell her what I had supposedly found out, which was probably kaka, and she did not feel obligated to pay me a cent. She was going to yoga. Don't bother to come by. She'd have her mind made up what to do by the time she'd taken savasana. Her whirling jags of words made me wonder if she had taken some savasana already.

Any embryo arena plans hatching in my right brain, an unstable nest even in normal times, aborted. "Face reality head on, for once, shithead," I said out loud. sounding a little like my mother, in principle at least. I had no money and my sister was flipping out, beyond PMS, into lithium or a divorce or both. I had to do something.

CHAPTER TEN

I heard Will and Enid laughing in the back bedroom. They jumped up when I walked in and yelled, "Come watch Nemo! Mama rented it for us." Only after we all settled on the bed did Enid, the quick one, say, "Why are you here, Uncle Sam?"

"Just dropped by. Any idea where your mom is?"

They shook heads, their eyes fixed on the shark dudes talking AA. They didn't seem to know she had left.

"Maybe in the basement." Will said. "She might be doing the wash."

I looked down the basement stairs. No lights, no chugging machine. She could be in Hawaii by now. How long had she been gone? I checked. They were about an hour into the video. I sat back down and tried to get into the little fish guy looking for his son. "Where's their mother" I asked.

"She's dead. A big fish ate her."

Not good. I got up. "Anyone want a sandwich or something?"

"We can't." Will gasped as a seagull crashed through a window.

"Sure you can. I'll make vegetarian, no cheese for you and no wheat for Enid, or vice versa. Whad'y want?"

"We can't. Mom said we could watch the movie but we could not get up, even to go to the bathroom until it was over. No eating." He pointed at a couple of scrunched cardboard cartons on the coffee table. "Only Juicy Juice. It's the rules if we rent movies. She said."

"Why?

"Because movies cost money and we don't want to waste any money not watching."

"Has your mother heard of Pause?"

The kids stopped wasting minutes listening to me. A fishnet writhed towards a blue girl fish. The kids breathed through their mouths in noisy gasps, not daring to blink.

This was what happened when you didn't let kids watch TV. When they do finally see a little, their brains seize. When he was about three, I babysat Will while Enid was being born, and because the Packers game was on, I tried to multitask. As soon as I said, "Watch that guy. He's the best." Will sat on my lap without moving for an hour and a half, except to ask, "We like the green ones, right?" When I told Sharon, she had a cow.

I sliced a couple of apples and we crunched our way to the ending credits. When they asked to see it again, I told them that their legs would dry up and drop off if they didn't get up and move. "Then?" they asked.

"We'll see," I answered, as I zipped up their jackets and sent them out the door. They ran down the walk and into the spandexed legs of their mother, frowning, her hair dark with moisture. "I told you not to move," she began, and then she saw me. "Go play with Justin. He's on his front porch dressing his cat. I'll call you when dinner is ready." Then she smiled at me.

"You're all wet."

"Bikram. Hot yoga. We shower afterwards." She looked me over. "What's your story?"

"Just the opposite. No shower." I followed her into the house. "So. What did you decide after taking sharvasa, or whatever?"

"Corpse pose. You lie down and empty your mind." She poured herself a glass of water, sipped it, looked at me. "It's harder for some of us than others."

She was trying to make a joke. A positive sign. "And?" I prodded.

"And I am going to trust Wilfred. I am not going to allow whatever is troubling him, including a bogus memory incident, to inflict itself on my belief in his integrity or, more important, on my idea of who I am." She raised her chin, looked soft-eyed somewhere behind me. "And," she met my eyes, not smiling, "I am sorry I pulled you into this situation. You have your own life to live."

My sister, my competent older sister was back. "This corpse pose. Just how do you do it?"

"You have to work up to it. You start by standing on your head."

"My emptier-than-yours head?" I wanted to hug her. Or maybe I wanted her to hug me. She did. And I asked, into her wet hair, "I'm still your brother, aren't I?"

"Of course."

"Then know that I want to be pulled into your life. And I will feel free to pull you into my life when I need you." Maybe soon, I thought. "If that's okay."

"First, we'll start with downward facing dog. Then, yes, for you we'll do warrior pose I and II, followed by a couple of twists to energize you and activate your kidneys. You look a little gray." Sharon finally smiled and I felt as if it was okay to leave. She hadn't paid me for my detective work, and I didn't remind her. Maybe neither one of us wanted to rock the steady boat we found ourselves rowing at that moment.

Back at my house, I cleaned myself up and took out my skates. They needed sharpening, but they were in good condition and I had time before my date with the ladies to borrow the machine at the arena and take care of them myself. In the meantime, I could read Allende or give Jack another go. I booted my hero up and reread what I had written. Jack needed to decide whether to call his ex-wife and go ahead with what might be the biggest mistake of his life, barring the marriage itself, or to reach out to the next possibilities, via another go at iMatch. The first alternative even Jack could see was stupid. The second offered a few possibilities. So I started typing.

Jack once again made contact with a woman, this time an artist, and she asked him to an art show, drinks after. He agreed to go, slicking his hair straight back like Jeff Bridges and wearing little round shades. His eyebrows no longer bothered him. She met him at the door of the gallery. Ten earrings encrusted her right ear and her hair was so acrylically black it seemed dangerous for her to be leaning over a candle, which she did as she poured him a glass of pale white wine. "Two buck Chuck," she said, "but okay."

My chair needed a pillow to support my back. My feet rested on a carton of computer paper, and my hands reached out in a casual way towards the keyboard. I closed my eyes, kept tapping at the keys.

The black-haired girl was too young for Jack, but her nipples, poking against the soft halter that dropped to her bejeweled belly button, invited him, scared him, actually. All that metal. Her (yellow?) black-rimmed eyes signaled she was waiting for something, waiting for him? Her hand cupped his buttock as they viewed the piece de résistance of the show, a nude Aphrodite in a warrior pose. "Quel magnifique! (or maybe "weird--" How does one say weird in French?) the black-haired girl murmured, squeezing a little and unsettling the crease in his carefully ironed trousers.

I was unsettling a little, too, as I clicked. Distracted, I took a break, and when I looked at my watch I saw it was five o'clock. So that's why writers write. A fugue, sort of, only with words. I opened a beer. The fugue lifted and I shut down the computer. I pulled a pizza out of the freezer, waited for it to bake.

Being Wednesday, TV was not an option, until l0:00. Okay, I told myself. It's Allende or nothing. I made it through the first thirty pages before I rescued the pizza and reached for Clive. Mom would have been proud.

On Thursday, I got my unemployment check, having applied for tech jobs in New York city the previous week and being disappointed as usual in the results of my applications. I paid my bills, bought some beer, and returned to Jack.

Jack had a good time, even though the black-haired girl sent him on his way after the show. She said, "Call me sometime." This was encouraging, but he noticed that she headed back to the gallery and started talking to a dude in a warlock outfit.

So, depressed, Jack decided to call his ex-wife. This is stupid, he told himself as he dialed. She was iffy, hesitated, then said that she'd meet him at Coffee Tyme that night. When he got there, he saw that she was sitting next to a dreadlocked guy who had his arm around her shoulders, a thumb edging southward. She introduced him as her guru, and she said Namaste, her bud of hands tucked between her breasts. The guy, Melvin, beamed at her and then at Jack. "Peace, " he said. Jack noticed that both of them are drinking something white. Chai. "Very spiritual," they said. As was the warm palm now on lying his ex-wife's thigh, he supposed. He ordered a double venti, full blast, and totally caffeinated, and as a result, was able to say, "Namaste to you too, Vicki. I'm outta here." He walked away feeling like a free man.

Too free. This was not where I wanted this story to go. I wanted Jack to discover that his ex-wife longed for him, wanted to make his life simple and content once more, like it had been. No hard times, then, that's for sure. Jack avoided them by going to Shaker's and watching Monday night football with his buddies. He rolled over them by calling his wife a bitch when she complained about the garbage, the yard, his skateboarding all weekend. At the end, he had lain subbornly flaccid under his wife's desperate hand and blamed her. He didn't know a hard time until it hit him in the face.

Whoo! Where did all that come from? I was suddenly sick of writing.

I lay down on the sofa, reached for an old *Esquire*, and flipped pages until the phone rang.

"Hello, Sam." Rose's voice was constricted, as if it was making its way through swirls of post nasal drip.

"Rose?" I asked to make sure. "What's wrong?"

"It can't be a fatal disease," she gurgled.

"Of course not. What are we talking about?"

"My novel. You were right. Too *Love Story*. But then what? I've spent two weeks trying to work it out. Maybe Mom's in love with a rock star? or pregnant? I can't make my fingers move."

I loved her snarly voice. I loved the fact that she called me, not Malcolm, at least that I was aware of. I could offer only one thing. "Come on over and we'll take a break. Maybe my mom has something that will inspire your muse to come forward."

"How poetic. What do you mean?

"Her third story." Then I remembered Sharon. She'd really be pissed if I didn't include her. "My sister, too."

I called Sharon. Yes, she'd get a sitter and bring ice cream. She sounded as excited about meeting Rose as reading Mom's story. I didn't ask about Wilfred.

I could tell by the way Sharon grinned at Rose that she liked her. They shuffled a little at the door, not knowing who was in charge of putting the carton of Cherry Garcia in the fridge, and then my sister handed it to Rose to let her know, I suppose, that her brother's girlfriend had precedence, kitchenwise. "You know about Mom?" she asked when Rose came back and settled on the couch.

"She was a writer. Still is, I guess, if you consider that she's still telling you stories. She must have been interesting."

"We just thought of her as Mom." I glanced at Sharon who was leaning towards the books as if they were whispering to her. "Still do." I pushed the button and the Mac lit up; a few seconds later the title of the third story popped onto the screen. "Here we go, her last attempt to get me to straighten up and fly right."

Sharon took a long pull on her beer, gave me her squinty sister look. "Why do you think this is all about you? This is about Mom, don't you see? She is telling us about herself, her thoughts, the parts of her we didn't know existed. "

I squinted back at her. "Didn't we decide that Mom did not have serial lovers, that these stories are fiction, figments of her imagination, like any other writer's?" I was thinking of Jack at the moment, but didn't want to go into my own figments.

Rose got up, stood behind me at the computer. "From what I can tell, imagination comes from somewhere inside a person. We don't create in a vacuum, do we? I don't."

"That's what I mean," Sharon said, poking me on the shoulder. "Mom was certainly not a vacuum." Before she could add her doubts about her brother, I scrolled into the story and we huddled in front of the screen, Rose on my knee, Sharon perched on the corner of my desk chair.

GETTING THERE

Even as he hunches under the car, his knee aching and sticking straight out in plain sight, his hip lodged against the rear tire in the way he has imagined it, Frank knows it won't work. Edie might be dingy, but she can still see.

As he expects, his wife comes thrashing around the back of the car, telling him to get up. "What are you doing?," she scolds, sounding like a mother again. "You're driving me crazy."

He considers the truth in that statement as he scoots his butt forward, dragging a leg along the driveway, and gets up on all threes, the bad knee not worth a damn. "I was checking the muffler."

"I could have run over you!"

He flinches as her boney knuckles whap the dust off his pants. That, of course, had been the idea, to get run over. Hearing his wife's ragged gasps as they walk up the path to the house, he knows he ought to tell her he's sorry, that he hasn't meant to frighten her, but then she'd ask why he did it in the first place. At the moment, the ache in his knee makes him think mostly about where he is putting his foot, and he can hardly understand it himself.

"It's okay, Edie," he says.

The sunlight hurts his eyes and he squints against it as they go into the house. In the kitchen, the usual foggy cloud in the center of his sight offers glimpses of the stove and fridge. He moves into the living room, finds his easy chair, drops into its familiar hug, and presses the lever that raises his legs up to where the knee no longer has any work to do. A stab of his finger brings on a slow parade of words from his latest tape, and he closes his aching eyes against the fluttering gray void and his ears to his wife's voice meandering in the kitchen.

Edie has always talked a lot. From day one, the minute he walked in the door after work, covered with gray overspray from the ships he was hired to paint and only wishing for a hot bath and the one drink he allowed himself, she'd start in, leaving him gasping, drowning in the trivia of her day. Somewhere along the line he learned that if he didn't meet her eyes, he wouldn't have to answer her. When their daughter Sarah was young, Edie had someone else to talk to, and the house took on a rhythm that did not include him. His fault, he guessed. "Your father's very quiet, that's all" he once overheard his wife tell Sarah as the two of them did the dishes. "Doesn't mean he doesn't love you."

These days, when Sarah stops by after work on Fridays, he can't hear a word she says as she kisses him hello, his blotchy vision obscuring all but a piece of hand or foot, his hearing aide useless in the muffled undertow of her words. Her voice was always soft, like a breeze, compared to Edie's hurricane. When the two women sit over coffee in the kitchen, their voices churning up the air between them, he's sure they still talk about him.

"Frank. I need for you to listen." Edie is shaking him, the tape turned off, a lamp lit over his chair. Her hand tightens his arm, her agitation quivering between her knee and his.

"I got lost."

"Yeh?"

"I had my appointment, you know, for Dr. Wilton. Because of that bump on my place down there. I told you about it. I got there okay, and then, when I tried to leave the parking lot, I couldn't think of which way. I went right and didn't recognize anything, so I turned around and went the other direction. Nothing. No Levenson's cleaners, where I always turn. No A&W. I turned around again and couldn't even find the clinic, just tall buildings."

"So you asked?" Frank knows she didn't.

"I pulled over and started crying."

"Yeh?"

"Then I stopped crying and told myself to get a grip."

He can imagine it.

"I saw the bakery. I saw the Doug firs behind it. I knew our house was under the trees. I just had to get to the trees. Then,," Edie sighs, "I found us!" Her hand leaves his arm, rests on her flat warm breast as she catches her breath.

Frank picks up his pipe, searches his shirt pocket for his lighter. "I keep telling you to write down street names." He considers adding that she should face it, she shouldn't drive any more, but she has gotten up, is leaving the room. His pipe whistles as he sucks on it.

"Don't you want to know what the doctor said?" She is standing beside him again.

"Sure." He takes a last pull on the pipe and brushes a hand against the singe he smells smoldering in his shirt front. He hopes that Edie won't notice.

"He said that I am dried up, and the bump is like a. . ." she hesitates, ". . .a callus, needs to be softened up."

"Callus."

"Nice young doctor, but a little rough, he said I should use a cream. . ." She holds up the box, aims it towards the edge of his eye so that he can see it. "Hormone something. I told him I was not into hormones. Look at my file, I said, breast cancer at 76, after a dose of hormones. Give me a break, I'm still feeling my boobs every day, but he said this was not the same, only makes the callus soft." She waits for him to say something.

"Sounds okay," he decides. What does he know?

"I'm glad about the cream," she answers. "Maybe it will help." Her voice is her young Edie voice, innocent, sexy, offering the world to him sixty years ago, offering only herself now. He almost sees the curve of her lips, her cheeks breaking into the soft ravines of a smile.

The horniness started last summer. She had slipped her hand between his legs in the middle of the night, whispering please, willing him to wake up. His penis, long unused to fingers other than his own, rose up, quivered and leaked, retreated and lay silent like the rest of him. Gently, she placed his hand on her body, and he searched with his fingertips for the wetness until she sighed and turned away. Lately, lying next to this new, restless Edie, he thinks what a cruel twist it is that a sad forgetfulness has brought her back to him.

Frank shifts his weight, tries think about something else. "So you're okay?"

"I just told you, didn't you listen?" Then she veers off in a new direction. "Time for dinner?" she asks.

"Or. . .?"

"Or lunch?"

"Look at the clock, Edie," he prompts, pointing at the mantle.

"Dinner, right?" She sounds pleased with herself.

"Right, dinner." No telling what she'll come up with to eat. She can't follow recipes anymore and every meal is a surprise. He sits back and presses the tape's green button.

"Chicken noodle," she says a few minutes later. "From a can." She arranges the tray at his side.

"I can still taste." He takes a bite of his sandwich, chewing it on the right side where he has the most teeth. If she's watching, she'll start in about dentures, he thinks, but instead she murmurs, "It's really weird. Maybe I am crazy."

"What?"

"I can't remember if I've had lunch, but just out of nowhere, I remember things, from a long time ago, like little movies except I feel them, like it's happening right now."

"Like what?"

"Like the time you cried."

He knows what's coming and tries to head her off. "When I saw Sarah the first time? You laughed at me."

"No, I mean later. You know. I just couldn't understand why you would do that, tell me you were going fishing and then be with that woman, that Janice."

"That was a long time ago, Edie." He, not Edie, has forgotten the woman's name.

"And when I asked you what was going on, you lied, said nothing was going on, but I knew, remember? I thought I would die."

"Edie. . ."

"I cried for a week, wondering what I had done wrong. And then one night, when you reached for me, I smelled her on you again. Remember?"

He does remember. "That was a bad time, Edie." He feels her get up out of her chair, kneel beside him, touch his temple, trace a finger like a tear down his cheek.

"We've had a good life, though, I think. Don't you?" Her hand travels across his chest, towards his belt.

He takes her fingers in his, presses them to his lips, catches the faint scent of the lotion she uses each morning. "A pretty good life," Frank says, surprised at the small jolt of pleasure these words give him. Forty years ago he couldn't have imagined it.

That night Edie had risen up from her pillow, her breasts sliding against the silk of her nightgown as she turned to him, her voice, low and foreign. "Why?"

He had thought of the way his body nearly exploded every time he knocked on that apartment door and heard that happy, "Frankie!" felt the warm arms around his neck. Like a young man. Like there was more to be had. Like he was still himself. But, at that moment, looking at Edie, at the pain reddening her eyelids, her trembling lips, he knew he would never be able to explain. When he wept, Edie believed it was because he was sorry he had hurt her and she held his cheek in her hand.

Her fingers slip away as Edie stands up. "Garbage day?"

"No, today's Tuesday, Edie."

They used to joke about it, the way people joke about dying or going bald or wearing diapers. "I've lost my keys again. Must be Old Timers," she'd say. He and Edie stopped laughing the day the empty pot on the burner burst into flames and turned the kitchen ceiling black with soot.

"I'm losing it," she said, and their doctor agreed.

Scribbling into his prescription pad, he added, "Might be years of good living yet," but Frank did not believe it, not the good living part.

Edie had always skittered about her days creating "what if's" and endless lists. "Take it easy," he'd tell her. "Life's too short." Her almost burning down the house changed that. From then on, he took over as worrier, his mind turning over the facts like puzzle pieces, looking for the one that would fit and bring some sense back to their life. This much he knew: his retirement check barely covered their bills and definitely would not cover the $3000 a month Old Timers were charged at assjsted living places, blind and deaf and no good to anyone. But their insurance policy was very clear. Demises paid $200,000. Suicide paid one-half. It couldn't look like he'd done himself in.

The car thing had been a bad idea, at least with Edie behind the wheel. He leans back into his lounger, closes his eyes, and puts his feet up as his wife clears away their dishes.

"I'm so glad you've decided to go out for walks," Edie says, her thin arm resting on his as they move along the sidewalk. He props his elbow against his hip, not sure who is supporting whom.

"Just remember to pick up your feet a little more so that you don't stumble. I wish you could see the Jensen's hydrangeas," she rambles on in her careless way. "They're bright maroon. Wonder what they put in the soil to get that color. Didn't you use to put nails under ours? What would make maroon?"

At the edges of the gray blot his vision of the world has become, he can see green grass, and tree trunks, and parked cars, or elephants, whatever. He spots the maroon.

"I don't know," he answers, thinking of their dog Buster, buried under the giant zinnias in the back yard. "Maybe old dog bones."

"We're at Second Street, already. Should we turn back?"

Her knowing the name of the street pleases him, makes him hesitate, and finally he is able to say, "Let's go across to the park." They have walked every day this week, and now, on Friday, the day he has chosen, his knee is killing him. Not enough, of course. That's the trouble. He wobbles a little over an uneven spot and Edie stiffens her hold on him.

"Are you sure?"

'Yep." He straightens his shoulders and raises his arm a fraction of an inch. He is as sure as he'll ever be.

"Next time we'll use your cane," she says. They stop at the curb.

The cars coming from the left do not enter his fringe of sight until they are almost in front of him and then they disappear. He takes his hand from Edie's arm and puts it into his pocket so she won't feel it trembling. When a green blur flashes at the edge of gray, he draws a quick breath. This is it, he tells himself, and he bends his good knee and plunges into the street. A swipe of metal throws him to the asphalt, a wail of brakes leaves him to understand that he is not dead yet.

Edie, clutching at his collar, keens softly into his ear.

Then, "My God! Dad walked right into my car." Incredibly, his daughter's voice, an anxious hearable screech, sweeps through him, a hand, hers, touches his forehead, dabs something at it. "What in hell was he thinking?"

Frank pulls himself up onto an elbow, probes at his bloody eyebrow with his fingertips. "I'm okay," he says, like always unable to explain himself. "Let's go home." He rolls onto his hip, gets his knee bent right and tries to rise up.

"Frank, don't. You might have hurt yourself." Edie still clings to him, pressing him down. Then her words are directed upward towards the shadow hovering above them. "This wasn't your fault, dear. My husband stepped right into your way. He doesn't see well, you know."

After a moment, Sarah responds in a calm undecipherable murmur, and he is lifted to his feet and led to the car. Doors slam, the motor rumbles, the car begins to move. Behind him, Edie leans forward, grasps the back of his seat, her words drifting in an anxious whirl past him, towards Sarah. "I feel as if I know you. Do you live near here?"

Frank closes his eyes, tries to imagine how it will go from now on. His daughter's hand brushes his thigh, remains there. He marvels at the comfort of her touch, and his fingers seek hers, entwine themselves with hers, and he gives himself over to her.

The women stood up, each reaching for her beer. "Damn.

This is too sad," Sharon moaned. "Trying to die and failing?"

"I don't think that's what it's about." I wasn't sure what I meant, but I was pretty sure that this was not a pessimistic story. "Maybe she was talking about--"

"Family, of course." Long tears trailed down Rose's T-shirt. "The web we are all caught in."

Sharon and I looked at her. She was crying and it wasn't even her own family. Nor ours.

"We wouldn't know," Sharon said. "Our family web blew apart years ago." I opened my mouth to disagree and couldn't think of what to say. Sharon looked at me. "Face it. We have a dead mother, a father who married a bimbo, and we are a brother and sister dangling like puppets in somebody else's hands." I guessed she was meaning those of a screwed-up husband. She shut her eyes, her lips moving silently as they did when she mantra'd out.

"Hey! I'm not dangling," I said. "Well, maybe if you mean from unemployment office hands." I laughed alone. Rose wiped her eyes on the back of her hands, Sharon stared at the books again. I didn't like idea of dangling. "I think you got it all wrong about this story. You said that stories don't emerge from vacuums, right? I think Mom was warning us. Remember Grandpa? That's who she was writing about. To warn us."

"Grandpa died when he was ninety, neither blind, nor deaf."

"And crazy as a jaybird, as Grandma used to say. Got lost climbing into bed."

"So Mom was telling us that we've inherited a genetic tic for Alzheimer's, and we should get ready? Wouldn't she have just told us?"

"I can't imagine Grandma Lilly and Grandpa Joe doing it. That's where the vacuum comes in for me." A similar vacuum, it occurred to me at that moment, had to do with my mother, same setting.

"God, you're so naive." Sharon turned to Rose as she put on her coat, "I like you. See what you can do with him." She surprised me by reaching for my neck, kissing my ear. "Read it again, Sam. And then we'll talk. About Mom's story. About the rest of it."

That kiss felt like family to me.

Maybe to Rose, too. "You're lucky to have her," she said as we sat back down on the sofa. Rose touched an ear, fingered a earringless ridge, explained, "I couldn't sleep on that side." She nestled against my shoulder, took my hand and massaged its knuckles. "The dangling thing. I never liked it either. I've always wanted to take my life in my own hands."

A stranger, rosemary scented, rubbed my palm, her thumb smoothing its lines, warming me all over. I touched my lips to the neat, brown part reaching diagonally across the top of her head. "Who are you?"

Rose sighed, moved in a little closer. "I'm just beginning to find out. I've always thought I was a writer, but I never knew for sure. My family, all strings and hands, especially my father, thought I should be an attorney. My mother objected. I had almost perfect SATs, could go to any school I wanted. Why not Harvard? Architecture, perhaps, or physics. She believed I could become a famous woman anything, if I tried. So I went to community college, majored in coffee drinking and poetry, moved out . . ." She paused, ". . .and lived with someone for a year."

"Malcolm, right?" I needed to hear it again.

Rose sat up. "Malcolm?" Her surprise dissolved into narrow-eyed disbelief, a lot like my sister's favorite nonverbal communication. "Malcolm!" She pushed against the seat cushion, trying to get up. I pushed her back down, said I was sorry, I was kidding. Of course, not Malcolm. But who?

"A musician, played guitar at nights, worked days as a rehab counselor. His band got a gig in Alaska. I didn't want to go to Alaska.

Instead I went to Brown and wrote my final thesis on Anais Nin, much to my father's horror." Rose glanced at the middle section of bookcases. "Did your mother read her?"

"I don't know. I'm still on the A's."

"Anais would have stood at the bedside and cheered your grandma and grandpa on, maybe even gotten in bed with them. She was an interesting lady."

"Like you." I was working on getting her ear down on my shoulder again, her hand anywhere. She stood up.

"I have to solve the fatal disease situation," she said.

I didn't want her to go. She would anyway. "Maybe it's not a problem," I said. "Maybe it's okay to die. It's not like you evaporate, you know. Parts of a person hang on for a long time."

Rose smiled as she closed the door. I went to the N shelf, found her, pulled out *A Spy in the House of Love, by Anais Nin . I was pretty sure it wouldn't be a cold war thriller.*

CHAPTER ELEVEN

Well, it depended on how one defined "cold," "war," and "thriller."

This was a story about Sabina who couldn't get enough, even though she had an understanding husband who took her back every time she returned from far-off acting jobs, whose plays were never reviewed, and for which she never needed to practice her lines. Cold, when you consider her use of the husband and his fat forgiving checkbook. The war part wasn't between her and her lovers: an opera singer who captured her fancy by singing Tristan and Isolde as she lay naked, suntanning on the beach; a pilot with whom she could relate on the flying part, only he meant one kind of flying, she another; and a wimp who could barely get his wrist straightened to touch her. The war was inside her. She either wanted to be a man, or not. Part of her wanted a man's freedom to fuck, release, disconnect and get back to work. But another part of her insisted that her role as a woman was to give, not to take. A virtuous wife. No wonder she ends up totally messed up and asking some weird stalker to set her free. He tells her she will be free when she loves someone. When she objects, says, "Hey, what do you mean? Look at all my affairs," he answers, "You haven't loved yet. You've only been trying to love, beginning to love."

I put down the book and considered that thought. For some reason I felt comforted. It made me a bumbler where Reba was concerned, not a shithead. I had tried, in my own hapless way, to love her. But I hadn't failed. I just didn't have enough practice, or wasn't ready, or maybe had some sort of love disability. I was only beginning to love, and whenever you begin something new, you fuck up once or twice. Maybe I never really loved Reba. And maybe I should stop feeling guilty about it.

I paged through the book again, rereading sections just for the words. Not pornographic. Erotic. Even I could understand the difference. I copied a paragraph, taped it on the computer to remind me what could be said:

> *"They fled from the eyes of the world, the singer's prophetic, harsh ovarian prologues. Down the rusty bars of ladders into the undergrounds of the night propitious to the*
> *first man and woman at the beginning of the world, where there were no words by which to possess each other, no music for serenades, no presents to court with, no tournaments to impress, and force a yielding, no secondary instruments, no adornments, necklaces, crowns to subdue, but only one ritual, a joyous, joyous, joyous, joyous impaling of woman on man's sensual mast."*

A great metaphor. A mast. I really liked it.

Then I remembered whose library this book came from. I couldn't put Mom and the word "impaling" in the same sentence. And how about Rose, the Nin expert? Men called it nailing. Women called it impaling. Obviously, the sex act implied violence. Aggressive, fueled by . . .as Anais would have said. . . passion. Banging. Forced entrance. Locked but yielding ramparts. Finally opening, what the fuck, who cares, because passion would get one past the gate. But not into the inner sanctum, the heart center of either the banger or the bangee.

Damn. I was spilling over with metaphors. Not as graphic as the mast, but maybe more true, if there are levels of truth. Up to now I'd only been learning to love, like Sabina. Barring the disability theory, I needed to keep practicing. Maybe I could find out what love really was. Maybe someday I would step into the traffic for my lover, like my mother's Frank.

And Mom? She knew how to love. Maybe what she didn't know about was sex. Maybe her search began at the beach house. And maybe she read Nin for inspiration. I'd never know. But she did turn down a couple of page corners, like she told me never to do to books, probably because she was in bed and didn't have a pencil.

Sometimes a person could overthink. I pulled on my coat and headed to Shaker's. The usual guys were there, except for Barney whose new girl had him by the balls, according to Jake, a fact confirmed by Todd and Davie.

We had gone to high school together, almost dropped out together. Actually Jake did drop out and got his GED a year later without opening a book. I was the first one to get hitched, and the other four were my groomsmen. None of us remembered much about the wedding except that we all woke up the next morning draped over the bed and the furniture of the hotel room that I had booked for Reba and me. I apparently would not let them go home in my condition. Reba was cool with that, tired, but excited to get to the Sunday brunch and the opening of the presents before we left for Tahoe and our short but sweet honeymoon. She told me she had rolled up in a comforter in the bathtub with the shower curtain closed so she wouldn't have to watch the various emptyings that went on all night. She was a good sport.

Davie was our leader, mainly because we could count on him always being at Shaker's after work, even though he had to be home to help put the kids to bed even on game nights. He made good money driving a UPS truck but he lost a lot of it betting on the games that filled the 50-inch screen on the far side of the bar. He played quarterback in high school and believed that if he had just gotten one break and had made it into Oregon State, he would have had a professional career. The break would have involved his 1.0 gpa morphing into a 2.5 gpa. It had happened for some guys.

Todd did go to college. He just got out a little early, encouraged by an administrator who gave him the choice of doing a little time or leaving and never coming back. That was during his growing years--twenty plants in the attic of his frat house. A brother narked on him after Todd wouldn't let him in on the enterprise. The night he was excommunicated, all of the brothers sat on their meeting room benches and hissed, probably to impress the alum representative. Todd slunk out, offering one last middle finger and a "Just you wait!" The next morning the brothers woke up to water seeping through the ceiling of the sleeping porch, across the floor, down the stairs, and out the front hall to the sidewalk. Todd had left his watering system on, a garden hose connected to a timer on an outside spigot, the only piece of evidence left at the scene of the crime, with nothing to water but the entire house. No one could prove that he had done it on purpose, and he came back to town and took a job in a nursery specializing in native plants.

Jake, with his brains and his GED, got into the ground floor of a company that developed specialized chips. He was still there, designing devices that I couldn't believe even when he explained them to me. All I knew was that in the near future my kitchen would ask me what I wanted for breakfast and I wouldn't have to steer my car, if I had one, ever again. Jake dreamed big, and I supposed that is what got him in trouble in high school.

"We thought you were dead or something." Davie looked me over, decided I wasn't, and went back to the game. Blazers and the Lakers. The Lakers were ahead, a fight looming, judging by the shoving and prodding going on in the backcourt. Todd waved a hand and signaled the bartender to bring me a Bud. Jake was drawing on a napkin, apparently not challenged by the action going on above his head. I sipped my beer and felt my backbone melt into the curve it always assumed at Shaker's. During a break, Todd leaned around Davie and asked what I'd been doing.

For a minute I didn't know what to answer. They all knew I was on unemployment, applying for jobs in NYC and glad I wasn't getting them, happy to spend my days hibernating. So it was a surprise to them, and to me, too, when I said, "I'm writing. Short stories."

Maybe I just needed to say I was doing something.

Whatever, they were having trouble saying something back. Finally Davie said, "Yeh? Well, you've had some experiences to write about." He added, "I guess," and the other two nodded.

"And you like to read. So it kinda fits." Jake lifted his pen from his napkin and thought about it.

Todd bent toward me, the only one showing a little excitement. "You know, I got a lot of stories in my head. I'm thinking of stories all the time, when I'm working or driving home. I just don't have time to write them down, you know? Maybe I could tell you some, you could write them, and we could share the profits?" He rocked on his stool, a story about to explode at any moment. From the size of his pupils, I could only guess the chemical source of his muse.

"Maybe next week, okay?" I offered. "I'm in the middle of something and don't want to get overloaded with ideas."

Todd turned his wide eyes to the game and stopped rocking.

All four of us drank and yelled and moaned as the Blazers, bullying their way to defeat, lost in the last minute to the Lakers.

We paid our tabs and wandered out into the street. It was ten o'clock. Davie had left at the third quarter, and the three of us mulled the possibilities--not many, on a Thursday, except maybe a meat market a couple of blocks away. Live music, maybe live women. I wasn't into even thinking about being a spy in the house of love after my bout with Anais, and I used my skating date with the old ladies in the morning as an excuse. "I'm getting back into skating," I said, turning and heading towards home. "Got to get up early."

When I got home the message light was flashing. "I just got a cell phone," Rose's voice said. She gave the number. "Call me. See if it works." I'd had too much beer to talk to her or anyone. I didn't call, even though the idea raised my mast a little.

The next morning, I got to the arena early and talked the Zam driver into letting me sharpen my skates. The ice, ready to sing, smelled so good I couldn't breathe deep enough to take it all in. I stepped onto it, stroked around its edges, remembered the first time I'd skated free. I was six and I had taken beginning lessons at the rink. My idea of skating focused on trying not to run into the boards or some other kid with sharp blades on his feet. Then the pond in the park froze over. It happened about once every seven years, and my dad walked me along the frozen path, with my guards on, to the edge of the ice. I stepped out, fell down, got up, and took off. A couple of other kids floated by, as mesmerized as I with the music we were creating. Great whoos rumbled under our feet, whoo, whoo, his whoo, my whoo, our whoos, filling my ears, my chest. I wanted it never to stop. But it did, of course, as more and more kids wobbled onto the pond, yelled, laughed, and absorbed the whoos. Once in a while, I had heard them again, on clean, clear ice, the sound reverberating against a high wooden ceiling. Like now.

The two women heard it, too. They didn't talk, just skated, inside and outside edges, around and around until they stopped, breathing hard, leaning against the boards. I stopped, too, and sprayed a little ice at their feet. We smiled, adjusted leg warmers-- in my case, unzipped a jacket. We began our separate exercises again, they probably imagining themselves as mature Michele Kwans, I resurrecting Bobby Clark and the Broadstreet Bullies. When the hour was up, we untied, and this time I accepted Mary and Jane's invitation to Starbucks for a cup of coffee. It was the first time I had ridden in a Mercedes.

They were nice women, about my mother's age when she died but crisper, as if they'd learned to speak from Katherine Hepburn, mouths set just slightly ajar, smiles twitching at the edges. Fingers touched hands and wrists, my arm, as we talked. No swear words, just rolling eyes to express dismay or frustration as we complained about Silver Skates.

"I've skated most of my life back East, outside, and I miss the breeze and the hot chocolate and the. . ." Jane paused.

". . .boys," Mary finished for her friend. "She got me into this by describing her girlhood on the lake, and despite the miserable state of the arena, I do love the exercise."

And I talked about my own singing pond and my hockey days, early on, then my teenage years when nothing else made sense. I didn't mention the reason I wasn't skating with the old guys lately, and under their kind, intense attention, I found myself expounding on my ideas of what a great skating facility could be. They listened and nodded. Then we said goodbye and I headed home. Jack was waiting.

CHAPTER TWELVE

So Jack, disappointed that his ex-wife Vicki had moved on to Melvin, decided that he needed to do what other men do, forget the love, go for the freedom of a relationship based only on sex. He called the black-haired girl again, whose name was . . . Anais.. .and is invited to her bed. She was an enthusiastic lover and he was a little overwhelmed at first by what she did and what she asked him to do. He caught on quickly, though, with the help of the illustrated books she kept by her bedside, and after a few visits, he found himself thinking of her constantly, wanting to be with her every night, and jealous and paranoid when she told him that she was busy. He dialed her number on those evenings and hung up when the recorder answered. Was she home, not answering because she was with someone else? Was she out with a lover, or a series of lovers? He couldn't stand the idea of another man paging through those books, or worse, not needing to. Finally, after a jealous frenzy of accusations in which he confessed that he loved her, Anais told him she was sick of him, of his constant need for reassurance, of his belief that love had anything to do with what they did in bed. He left, told never to come back.

I clicked on Save and Quit, and got up. I had left the sex scenes blank until I could find a copy of *The Joy of Sex* and do a little research in the *Kama Sutra*. Nin was way too girly to use as a reference for Jack's sex life. I glanced at the bookcases and knew Mom wouldn't help me out either, unless she had disguised her sex guides in innocent book jackets to keep us kids from reading them. She probably did.

I called Rose on her new cell phone, but it was turned off. Why did a person have a cell phone if she left it turned off? Then I was glad I couldn't talk to her because I would have asked her for a couple of books she probably had on her shelves. I didn't want to know about them yet.

Wilfred had requested a couple of days. It had been a couple of days. I called my sister's house but no one answered. Hockey practice, I guessed. I left a message and hung up. When I called Wilfred at his office, his receptionist said he was out for the rest of the afternoon. Did I wish his voice mail? No, I answered, I'd be seeing him over the weekend. And he'd better have a good story.

It was Friday afternoon, time for my date at the unemployment office. I left the house antsy, like I was breaking out in scabies, and for the first time, I felt a little guilty about applying for impossible jobs. Maybe I should get serious. The idea made me even more uncomfortable. I couldn't think of one job I would qualify for except Zamboni driver. I would make a terrible waiter. I didn't like taking orders from anyone, even customers. The arena nachos taught me that.

By the time I got to the office, I itched all over and almost didn't go in. Instead of going to the computers, I headed toward a frowning woman sitting at a desk under a sign reading "Job Counseling." Couldn't hurt. I sat down in the chair her eyes directed me to. She was talking into one of those little black wires that McDonalds drive-up servers use. "You'll need to come into the office," she was saying. "It's impossible to evaluate a resume on the phone." She listened for a minute, said, "I can tell you without seeing it, however, that six pages is too long. Bring it in. Or get it to one page. Or both." She stopped frowning. "You're welcome." She nodded at me, "You're lucky. I've had a line of ten people all morning. I'm Mrs. Jensen. How can I help you?"

"I need a job, but I don't know what I want to do." Pathetic.

"Okay," she answered. "Let's find out," like she had heard my problem before. "Let's start at the beginning." She took out a notepad and began asking questions.

By the time her curiosity was satisfied, a line of other apparent scabies victims was writheing behind my chair, and my mind had been reamed. She wrote down the dates and times of a couple of tests, and told me I needed to go to a class, a group, really, as if that made a difference, where folks discussed job issues and got resources. "I don't suppose you have a resume," she said, and when I shook my head, she signed me for that class, too. "Don't bother applying anymore in New York," she said as I got up and remembered to shake her hand. "Neither the Rangers nor the Islanders need a right wing." She handed me a piece of paper that got me next week's check without the eastern connection. "And *The New York Times* is fresh out of openings for sports writers. Good Luck," she said, and I believed she meant it. A light flashed on her desk, and she replaced her headset and frowned over the mouthpiece. I walked away hoping I'd get to talk with her again. It felt good to be listened to that way.

I felt good again when I got home and saw the light on my phone blinking. Rose had called. "I saw you on my caller ID. I was writing," she said. "I turn it off when I'm working."

"It's Friday," I answered. "How about Italian and a movie?" As I spoke these words, it occurred to me that I didn't know what she liked to eat, one, and, two, what she liked to watch. If I was to begin to learn to love, I'd have to start inquiring rather than assuming.

"How about mu shu," Rose answered, " and a little poetry? At my place." She apparently was not bothered by my assumptions. She rolled right over them. I said great, although I had no idea what mu shu might be. Or poetry, I realized.

"Bring something to read to me. See you at seven."

A poetry reading. Out loud. I thought about bringing the quote hanging above my computer, the Anais Nin thing, but I figured that something like that would take weeks, maybe months, judging from our progress so far, to be applicable. In grade school I had to memorize "Paul Revere's Ride," but Longfellow was as wrong for this as the mast was. Mom liked poetry, quoted it once a while: "Be up and be a' doing with a heart for any fate," when she wanted to make a point.

I went to the book cases. The poetry books were the skinny ones, mostly, and I pulled a few out. I liked the title of the first one, *Songs of Innocence*, like it might fit our situation, but lambs seemed to be the main characters, maybe because it was written in 1789. The next book was written by an Irish guy who advised me to never give all of my heart in one poem and in the next, to spread my dreams under my woman's feet to be stepped on. A little masochistic, I thought. I kind of liked one where he compared a "her" to Helen of Troy who filled his days with misery. I put a yellow Post-it on it.

A couple of the poets were too female for me. Maybe Rose could relate to them, a mother trying to kill herself, writing her four-year-old daughter all about it. And the dark one telling of blood and children dying in Viet Nam, and wells of salt brimming, forcing out the poems. Maybe later.

The insides fell out of the next book, like Mom had worn it out. l978. Twenty five years ago, a couple of page corners turned down. *Geography III* by Elizabeth Bishop. These poems told long stories. The first had a little girl sitting in a dentist's office looking at a *National Geographic*, discovering she is like everyone, even the women with the sagging breasts. The moment passes. The war is still going on, l9l8. The next poem is in the mind of Robinson Crusoe after he gets back to England. He misses Friday and his other island. The best one, the one I will read, I decided, is about a moose, no, actually, about strangers who experience joy, the human connection, when a moose crosses their path.

I flipped through a couple more books, sniffing at the words, wondering why I had thought I didn't like poetry or couldn't understand it, although I did find quite a few I didn't want to spend time with. Then I opened the last book and met a guy named Billy, not William, Collins and very funny, in a truthful kind of way. I read the first poem, about why he didn't keep a gun in the house, involving a barking dog, and I didn't stop until I get to the last one where he confessed he had a crush on me, his reader.

I arrived at Rose's with Elizabeth and Billy in hand, a bottle of white wine and a six-pack of Coors, just in case. In case of what, I wasn't sure, but I was grinning, showing all my teeth, when she answered the door. She showed me hers, too. Why humans do that, the teeth thing? Then I wondered if I would have thought that thought if I hadn't spent the whole afternoon reading similar wonderings. Rose interrupted my musing by taking my coat and hanging it in a closet, putting the wine in the fridge and motioning me to her futon.

She'd straightened her apartment. Books were stacked under reading lamps. The wastebasket was empty. Neat lines of Post-Its fringed the monitor of her word processor, the desktop coffee-cup-ring free. "You've painted or something," I said. Green walls lapped at my skin, made me want to sink back, not move.

"Celadon," she answered. "Chinese. Good feng shui, brings the body and soul closer."

I heard myself sigh.

"Let's start with the beer," she said. "We're going to get thirsty." Of the three books piled up on the coffee table, I recognized two. The female ones. "Anne Sexton," I said. "I've read her. She seems so . . ."

Rose looked at me, an eyebrow arched like my mother's would have been. "Unstable?"

"Open. She doesn't hold back, does she?"

"Did she. Maybe not holding back, just staving off the demons." Rose settled into her corner, cross-nlegged, propping the beer bottle in her crotch as she leaned forward and took a book from the table. "So how else are you going to surprise me tonight?"

And we began. She read and then I read. Three times around. When I heard her voice, her slow, deliberate mouthing of those women's words, images swirling by, I could imagine Rose, my sister, my mother at their desks, pens cutting through the silence. When I read about the moose, about the dentist's office, I could imagine me dragging small moments across a page, fingering them, trying to find the chewable nuggets. We ended with Billy eating his osso bucco, teaching his poetry workshop, telling us about his dog. We drank another beer and Rose asked when I had taken a poetry class and I said this afternoon. Then it felt like it was time to read one more poem and I chose Billy again:

The valentine of desire is pasted over my heart
and we are not touching, like things
in a poorly done still life
where the knife appears to be floating over the plate
which is itself hovering above the table somehow.

Rose went to her desk, pulled out a book. "I hadn't meant to do this." She read:

Not dead of wounds, not born
Home to the village on a litter of branches, torn
By splendid claws and the talk all not of villagers,
But stung to death by gnats
Lies Love.
What swamp I sweated through for these years
Is at length plain to me.

"Edna St. Vincent Millay," she said. "A woman with her own ideas of love."

I knew Billy or Elizabeth or even Edna would have something I could thrust into this sparring, but I was suddenly not wanting to duel. One afternoon does not a poet make. I swallowed the last of my beer, fell to one side, lay my head in Rose's triangle of body and legs, and said, "I give."

"One more. No gnats. Only a toad." Her fingers threaded my willing hair. This poem she knew by heart.

Somewhere this dusk
a girl puckers her mouth
and considers kissing

the toad a boy has plucked
from the cornfield and hands
her with both hands;
rough and lichenous
but for the immense ivory belly,
like those old entrepeneurs
sprawling on Mediterranean beaches,
with opened eyes,
it watches the girl who might kiss it,
pisses, quakes, tries
to make its smile wider:
to love on, oh yes, to love on.

"Galway Kinnell," she murmured as she leaned forward, her breasts like muffs against my ears, her mouth upside down catching my bottom lip in a wet slurp, a teeth clashing, until I whirled on the axis of our connected lips, my legs flailing above the mattress, my hands searching for a neck, a hold on a nobby back bone, finding finally a part of her, warm as bread.

"Are you all right?" she asked. She unfolded herself, straightened out against me. My head had worked itself under the wooden arm of the futon.

"Let's move down a little," I whispered, and we did, and her T-shirt stayed where it had been, my fingers traveling the trail of ribs to the ring at her navel.

They asked a question, apparently, because she answered, "That's the only one. Unless you . . .?"

Then we didn't talk for a while. Her skin stretched silkily over ribs, hips. My hands wandered across a breast, nipple stirring, pausing at the elastic edge of her panties, entering the crease below that edge where my palm fit into the curve of her spine. I was surprised how small she was, how fragile her breath at my neck. I thought I might hurt her, roll over on her, flatten her against the mattress's rough cotton. I slipped my arm under her neck, bent into her breasts, kissed her along a sensuous garden path until my lips met the bejeweled ring. I took it between my teeth, lifted my head to take a breath.

"Yikes!" Her hand shoved against my ear. "You're supposed to lick it or something." She pulled her shoulders away from me, looked down. "My God, I'm bleeding."

We sat up, both of us pink-cheeked and squinting. "I guess this isn't the moment to discuss Anais Nin, is it?" I pulled her shirt down and dabbed its hem at the drops of blood gathering in her navel. Her stomach roiled like a pot of oatmeal. I put my hand on the roils, looked up and saw that she was laughing, or crying, maybe both, her hands covering her eyes -and water seeping between her fingers.

"Oh, Rose. Oh, Rose." I moved my lips towards those salt paths. My tongue swabbed the drains, the v's between the fingers, the leaking eyelids. Rose stopped heaving, tremoring more softly under my tongue. I kept licking, searching for salt, for the faint trail of rosemary I was following as I traveled downward through the valley of breasts with their hard little sentinels, their hidden arroyos, the plains leading to that well of blood and jewel, where I kept licking until Rose's hands again stopped me, this time to loosen her belt, my zipper, a condom, our bodies.

Between the two of us, we didn't find a need for the Kama Sutra that night, just a bandaid, when it was all over and we could laugh again. I didn't think I'd ever laughed during sex before.

Like us, the mu shu was messy. The scent of white wine, of Chinese pancakes, of our bodies, befogged us. I left promising to read a few pages of Louise Gluck, tucked under my arm, before I went to sleep. I didn't, of course. Clive Cussler and I spent an hour or two chasing the bad guys and even at that, I woke up earlier than I had in months, thinking it was time to be up and be a'doing, with a heart for any fate.

I needed to work on a couple of unfinished projects. The first was my sister's marriage, a rollercoaster car careening out of control. The second involved my entire life, also out of control. The first seemed easier. I called Wilfred at his office, told him it was time to come clean, not to me, to his wife, who didn't deserve to go through life hanging on by the tips of her nails. To my surprise, he agreed. "I want you to hear, too. I'll pick you up in a half hour." He sounded as if he hadn't shaved for a couple of days.

CHAPTER THIRTEEN

Wilfred's car sidled up to the curb in front of my house; the lock of the passenger door clicked a welcome, and we drove away without talking. He could have been sitting for a portrait: the brows furled, the chin, newly shaved, I noticed, squared to meet the next challenge. His arms, if he hadn't been driving, would have been hidden behind him, fingers entwined. Instead, they clutched the wheel, a trail of NPR classic music massaging them. We pulled into the driveway and got out. I wondered if Wilfred had checked whether Sharon would be home.

She was. One leg skewered the air, the other was planted on a purple rubber mat. An arm waved unsteadily at the ceiling, her horizontal torso raised and strong on a quivering wrist. "Ardha Chandrasana," she said, greeting us as we walked into the entry. "I'll be down in a minute."

The coffee pot was on and Wilfred shook his head when I pointed at it, then nodded yes as I poured. I thought he probably needed a shot of Chivas instead of decaf, but he sipped at the cup, then put it down and lifted his chin as he waited for his wife to come through the door. For a moment, I admired him. Then I remembered that he was about to bring my sister 's life crashing down around us and I hated him. Then I realized that this was not my business. I was here to pick up the pieces once this conversation was over.

I pushed out of my chair and stood up. Wilfred said, "Stay." So I did.

Sharon joined us. A runoff of sweat darkened the center of her jersey to her waist. Moons seeped southward under her arms. Her forehead shimmered. "That felt good!" she said. "So. . . ." She held a bottle of water over her mouth, allowed it to gurgle as she swallowed . . . ."What?" Even wet, she looked good, blonde and confident in a high-cheeked, hands-on-hips way.

Wilfred cleared his throat, then raised his eyes to hers. "First, I love you. No, don't say anything. I need to tell you that, and if I have hurt you, it's not because I don't love you."

Sharon frowned, nodded, wiped a drop of water from her chin, sat down.

"A couple of months ago, I got a call from the police. Angie had given them my name. She told them I was her only relative. She had been found beaten, raped, and almost dead, not from the beating but from an overdose of heroin."

Angie, Wilfred's first wife was a sick person, Wilfred had explained years ago, but he hadn't said it in a divorced way, more like he was sad. Maybe he was, even after he married Sharon, for a while at least. Sharon had told me that early in their marriage Angie called often, talked to Wilfred, asked his advice. Sharon decided that this connection was simply a remnant of Wilfred's past, and when he hung up and looked out a window, she would hug him, tell him she understood. That was at first. After the kids came, the calls stopped. Now, I saw my sister biting a lip, holding steady.

"Why you?" she asked.

Wilfred shook his head. "I don't know. At least, I didn't know. I went to the hospital, found out she'd been living on the streets, selling herself to buy drugs. A john beat her up." His lips trembled and he pressed them into each other. "I didn't recognize her. She had become a gray skeleton, thin bruised arms, dark circles under her eyes. . . ." He hesitated. "The doctor said she needed to go into treatment. He suggested the city facility for indigents. Two weeks for drying out, then out-patient sessions for a few months. When he said that, Angie said, 'I did that. Twice. Help me.'

"Sharon, I should have known where she was headed fifteen years ago when I found her stash of pills. I got angry then, and every other time I found out she was still using. Then she left. And ever since, I've felt guilty. Every phone call reminded me how much I'd failed her, had not understood what it was like for her. I couldn't fail her again. I promised I would help her."

"So you set her up in a fancy rehab center, spent your savings and didn't bother to tell your wife? Why the hell not?" I wanted to grab him by his silk necktie and strangle him.

Sharon, though, seemed to be on the verge of a smile, her hands gathered in her lap. "Because he wanted to rid himself of her." Her voice was calm, cool. "Remember Mom's story, Sam? The lingerie, the yelling? That was about Angie. She surfaces every once in a while like a dead body and Wilfred leaps in and tries to resuscitate her." She looked at her husband, said, "Did it work this time? "

Her husband brought a gold ringed hand to his eyes. "Oh, God! Sharon. I'm sorry."

"Did it?" Sharon asked, still not moving, just watching.

"I chose Honeywell House because it was the best rehab in the state. I took her in and paid upfront, the first $l0,000. She asked me to help her do it, and I told her I'd come as often as I could. Angie had some very bad days-- and nights. I sat with her, read to her, watched her vomit, held her arms when she seizured. She settled down after two weeks. Then one day she walked out of the center and disappeared. I was frantic, angry. I found her hours later at the hotel where she kept a room. I brought her back and stayed with her until I could trust her. After a second payment and a couple of weeks, her therapist says she's over the worst part. Angie's talking about going back to her hometown in Iowa, making peace with her parents, beginning again."

"And you didn't tell me because. . .?"

"I thought I should do this on my own. It was my problem. I had to deal with it. I couldn't hurt you again like I did before, allowing her to come between us."

"And you think she hasn't?" My sister's folded hands lay in her lap.

"Sharon, I don't believe I ever loved Angie, even in the beginning. We got married because she needed me. She was like a wounded bird. I liked being needed, but it turned out I wasn't up to it. I didn't know what to do with a wife who was sick and crazy."

I could relate to that. I myself hadn't known what to do with a wife who was perfectly sane.

"I know more about love now. I should have trusted you from the beginning, trusted that you would understand. I'm sorry I didn't." Wilfred reached out, took one of Sharon's quiet hands. "But I've learned so much from you in the past weeks. And I've learned that I love you more than I ever thought possible."

That was my signal. I stood up, headed for the door. Neither of them answered my "See ya."

I wished I had a can to kick as I walked home, my mind kicking its own can, jumping curbs, getting stuck in hedges. If I could judge by my sister's marriage, people who really loved each other stayed together, no matter what. But my parents hadn't. Reba and I hadn't. And we all believed we loved each other for a while. So maybe it wasn't love, maybe it was something else that held two people together for the long run, some sort of stretchy band of respect, or gratitude, or maybe a vision of old age with grandchildren and a life different from the first messy years when the Shoulds rattled and scraped against each other.

My grandmother Lilly had a butcher knife that ended up at the estate sale less than a half inch wide, my grandfather had sharpened it so often in the 56 years they were married. Maybe relationships work the same way, the rough places honing the edges, keeping them keen and vital. A poem leaped between my can-kicking thoughts:

Our edges are sharp,
My wife and I,
A set of tools at the ready.
She fillets
I chop chop
Our stomachs hold the table steady.

Damn, I'm good, I thought, as I opened my door. Not Edna St.

Vincent Millay, of course. I decided to call Rose, recite my poem, let her know what had gone on at Sharon's. I was distracted by the blinking light on the phone. Maybe she had called me.

I picked up the message and heard my sister's cool voice. After I left she had asked Wilfred to move out. He was packing his bags as she spoke. "I will no longer live with a ghost in my marriage bed, huddled between my husband and me. I've tried, but it's too crowded. I can't breathe. Perhaps you can understand, Sammy. Thanks for trying to help."

I hung up and didn't call Rose. I wasn't sure I could make words come out of a throat so tight I couldn't swallow. I sat down and tried to think. Wilfred had stepped over a line Sharon had drawn. Was it the confession I heard? Or after I left, had he uttered one more sentence, a sentence that sent him out of bounds and out of his marriage? Or maybe reality took a little time to harden into a truth, like the spread of water over ice. Sharon was skating away, leaving behind a husband hanging onto the boards. At least, after that speech about loving her, he should be. But maybe he wasn't. Maybe he went directly to Honeywell House and into the arms of his recovering ex-wife, the two of them needing each other so much it seemed like love again. I couldn't stand that idea, a familiar, used-up one, the one I used to cling to after Mom and Dad broke up when I believed that somehow my parents would learn to love each other again because we needed them so much, and we would once more march along through life in tandem.Instead, we went on to follow four separate paths, each in a different direction, mine, in an aimless circle, the others towards the next place: Mom, independent, writing and traveling; Dad with Janelle; Sharon, the supermom and wife. But now even her trail had forked.

"God, Sam. Stop and listen a minute." Rose sat cross-legged, looking into my eyes which were trying to blink her into a soft focus. "Your metaphor is faulty. Or at least weak, when it comes to families. A family is not on some sort of road through life together, all aiming to end up at the same place. Only Mormons believe that, and even they lose it when they try to explain where the wives and husbands of all the children fit in into their heavenly home."

I had called her and she had brought chai, which was making its way down my throat in a soothing way, between gulps of salty mucous. I couldn't seem to stop draining, the ache having made its way to my chest. I accepted the wad of toilet paper Rose had unfolded herself to get for me.

After I blew, I asked, "What?"

Rose knew what I meant. "Most families, except really dysfunctional ones, are more like trees. They have a trunk, a sturdy early history, but as time goes by, they branch out, limbs reaching in all different directions. And those limbs separate. The leaves bud out on the branches, the young ones. No, don't say anything, I'm working on this. The branches become limbs, which send out their own branches. After forty years, the trees are huge, complicated, have had some wind damage, have produced any number of fruits or nuts, each part doing what it is supposed to do at a certain time of the year or life. "

"Your point?" My eyes had dried up enough to see her holding up her hand to demonstrate.

Rose frowned, brushed back her hair. "Think about it. If your parents hadn't divorced, if decisions to change hadn't been made, you could be living with your father and spinster sister in the family home with the curtains drawn in respect for your dead mother, who never did get a chance to write."

"A little harsh," I said. But I guess I was getting the arboretum picture. Decisions were branches, not dead ends. Every tree had them, needed them and when leaving the security of the trunk, every new thrust was filled with unknowns. "Leaves are the good parts," I said.

Rose's misty lips curved at me.

"I think you are a leaf," I added.

Her body leaned in and she said, "I think so, too, so stop leaking, Now that we've got the metaphor corrected, let's move on to a non-verbal kind of communication."

"Call your sister," she said as she left a while later. "She'd like to hear from you. It's the tree thing to do." She kissed me on my throat where I still was getting hits of sadness. I wanted her warm lips to nestle under my chin all night. "Next time," Rose promised. "I'm editing my novel, line by line. It's like pruning a bush. You have to go slow."

Trees, bushes, leaves. Families, work, love. I realized I had forgotten to recite my poem to Rose. About knives. Perhaps it was good that I hadn't. I needed to call Sharon, listen, not talk.

CHAPTER FOURTEEN

Sharon wasn't home. Or at least she wasn't answering her phone. If she didn't call back in the morning, I'd go over after my class at the employment office, maybe take the kids skating after school. I hated to think what they were feeling right then. I hoped Sharon had told them that Daddy was off on a trip or something, but knowing her, I knew she hadn't. She'd sat them down and told them the truth. As she saw it, of course. And they would have been confused, just like I was. He said he loved her; she had said she loved him. And everybody had ghosts, right? I used to think of Reba as a splinter lodged in my heart. Maybe that's what Sharon was talking about when she said I would understand. Because of Rose, the splinter had dissolved. Reba was still a part of me, though, like a small sometimes-itchy scar, or the rustle of memories that cluster at the edges of sleep.

I'll talk to Sharon about ghosts, I thought; how they linger to instruct us, to remind us of past decisions, to point a vaporish finger in the next direction. Let Angie's ghost settle in for the long haul, I'd say. She may turn out to be your best friend, I'd tell her, reminding you that your prick of a husband has a human side, is able to cry, say I'm sorry, do penance, and, most important, love. Inside the covers of his constant day planner. he has recorded his unplanned days, Angie's first call; unfamiliar telephones, addresses, the websites, times to visit, places to find her, a day totally wiped out, circled hockey games not to be missed, no matter what was going on elsewhere, but missed anyway. Love of a kind, uninvited, feeding on regret and lost chances, but love. Someday Sharon will be glad her husband could reach into himself, pull out the courage to face this kind of love, do something to assuage the guilt that he's kept at bay all these years, admit to caring about Angie, her tumultuous life.

That's what Angie's ghost teaches, I'd tell her. Because you got it right, she really is a ghost. Neither dead nor alive. Not a part of Wilfred's life, with no substance in his real world. You said he was trying to rid himself of her. I think it's more that he is trying to find a place for her, a safe place where her memory can curl up and doze off. You can't kill off ghosts. Even when you get married to exorcise them, they hang around. Even when you get so busy you can't read the scratches in your Day Book, they linger between the lines. And when you look the ghost in the eyes and say I'm sorry, it asks for a place to settle in. Might as well make peace with this ghost, Sharon, I would say.

I rehearsed this lecture as I waited on the couch for my sister to return my call. Like Mom said, the words billowed from some place inside me. I couldn't hold them back or figure out where they came from, they just needed to see the light of day. Who would have thought?

The words didn't always billow for my mother. I was fifteen, a bad year for kids. I had told Mom I was going to a football game. Instead, I ended up in the back seat of Stella's car. She was sixteen. We did it. She drove me home. I slipped past my parents' bedroom, hoping they'd not hear me, but the door was open, a light on. When Mom saw me, she said, "Hello, Sam. Better late than never," I had to show my face. I pulled my shirt down over my fly and whatever evidence might be lurking there, and said, "Hi, where's Dad?" It wasn't like him to be gone on a Saturday night.

"Come, sit."

My mother's eyes red, her face spongy, unfamiliar. A lank hand plunked against the quilt. "Here," she said.

I stepped into the room, perched on the edge of the bed out of that hand's reach. Somehow she knew about tonight; maybe she was the person who had walked by whistling, and Stella had said shush and pulled me flat against her. A hot rise of anger made me say, "What?" She had no right to care so much.

"Your father has left us." I could barely hear the words as they slid through dry, still lips.

"What?" I repeated.

She turned toward me, her leg nudged my hip. "He's left the house." Her shiny eyes searched, found mine. "He has met a woman he cannot live without."

I breathed against the tightness of armor I must have been forging for as long as I could remember, for just that moment.

"I'm not surprised, Mom." I heard myself say. "You and Dad are really different people." My response, so solid, so manlike, pleased me.

My mother lay silent, unmoving. Stunned, I thought, at my words. Then she smiled. "Out of the mouths of babes," she said.

It was going to be all right. I kept talking. "You're young, you know. There are lots of rich old geezers out there, looking for someone like you. You won't be alone long."

This time she laughed. Then I kissed her on her hot cheek. "It's going to be okay."

I got up and left, her reading light still on, a faint I love you , Sam, following me down the hall. I got into my bed and lay there forever, my legs itching, jerking against the sheets to rid themselves of the bugs crawing under my skin. Sleep was impossible. How had I known this would happen? What had I done to hurry it along? Why wasn't I blinking away tears? I couldn't think in answers, only questions. Finally I got up and crept downstairs, past the dark door of my mother's room, to the kitchen where I knew a bottle of bourbon was stashed in the liquor cabinet. It was empty. I had to settle for red wine.

Mom and I both slept in the next morning. After we got through the Sunday comics and our separate favorite sections of the newspaper and a pot of coffee, I said, "Now what?"

Mom got up, cleared the table. "Sharon will be home this afternoon from her senior sleepover at the beach. Your father will be here at 5:00 to talk to you both about what's happening. Let's pick up the house." Mom was still a little puffy, but if she had emptied the bottle, she should have been. I had a headache. I hated red wine.

She paused at the door. "By the way, Sam. This doesn't make you the man of the house now. I am. Try not to forget that in the next few months. We still have a curfew, which you broke last night. Don't do it again." Then Mom must have decided it was not the moment to exact consequences because she added, "I did, however, much appreciate what you said. Although, I think when the time comes, I'll not opt for rich old geezers. A soft touch is what I'll be looking for."

I thought I knew what she meant. "That's good, Mom, especially if he's rich," I said, a pile of newspapers in my arms. "We'll have a maid."

Now, years later, I reconsidered that conversation. It was possible that my unexplainable, obnoxious behavior as a teenager did not destroy my parents' marriage. That they themselves destroyed it; that I was a product, not the machinery, in a malfunctioning union. That Mom was as dissatisfied as Dad.

Soft Touch. The book rested between *The Pleasure Principle* and *Inner Tennis* in Mom's non-fiction section where I had shelved it in the nonfiction G's. I pulled it out and flipped through a few chapters. Then I paged through *The Pleasure Principle*. Erotic, both of them. I was becoming well-versed in the genre. "Some of the names of authors are real, some invented," an editorial note indicated on the last pages of *The Pleasure Principle.*_"Unsigned" had written half of the stories in *Soft Touch*. And in each book, a star appeared in the margin next to one of the titles, its blue ballpoint ink fading against yellowing pages.

Did the stars indicate that my mother, as "Unsigned," or "Susan Van Brick" had written a couple of the stories, about cunts, about suave cocks, about frangipani branches pressing into buttocks? My mother, who at the same time was reading my discarded Louis L'Amours, and who, I reminded myself , also wrote the first of the three stories on my computer.

Fifteen years ago, she dyed her hair reddish brown and wore teacher clothes during the day, ear-ringed and skirted. At night and on weekends she'd pull on worn jeans and clean the house and garden and go to my hockey games, sitting next to my father if he showed up without Janelle. The two of us ate dinner together when our schedules allowed it, and she taught me how to drive. One New Years Eve when a party went bad, she picked me up at a hospital after a couple of us had somehow gotten Davie the emergency ward. I didn't doubt that she'd be there when I called . She brought me home, then gathered up a champagne bottle and two glasses from the coffee table as I headed up to bed. I remember saying, "Hope I didn't interrupt anything," and not meaning it.

I never worried about her. She had friends. She played tennis and went out to faculty parties and sat around in the living room drinking wine with the neighbors who chose her instead of Dad to associate with. She had a job full of kids worse than me, principals worse than Dad, to occupy her time, and it didn't occur to me to wonder how my mom spent the Saturday nights I was spending somewhere else.

I did meet a couple of guys she went out with: one, a rounded belt-strangled belly; the other, ancient white hair straggling against a shirt collar; a third who tried to sell me life insurance while he waited for her to come downstairs. We'd talk about them the next morning and she'd say she was still looking for a frog to kiss. I told her to keep turning over rocks, he's bound to show up any day, relieved, I guess, that my life wouldn't be changing.

But it did. I was seventeen, thought I knew it all, wanted to be free to live my own life, play hockey, fuck, drink, smoke a little, and work on my car. School was a joke. One night I got ahold of a couple of porn tapes and invited Jake and our girls over for beer and laughs. The tapes were so terrible that at first all we could do was laugh, but then the room got quiet and we got into the spirit of the thing. Jake and Steph pumped on the sofa, Erin and I grabbed a pillow and handled each other on the floor in the blue light of the TV. I had most of her undone when the front door flew open and the overhead light shocked us into sitting up, fumbling with buttons, squinting.

My mother stood in the entry, hands on hips. In the background the tape squealed and grunted. She took a deep breath and said, "Get out." The fling of her arm included me. "Take your clothes," she said, pointing in my direction. "You don't live here any more."

I stumbled up the stairs, filled my hockey bag with whatever I found in my drawers, grabbed my music tapes and a book from the bed table, remembered a tooth brush and a jar of Vaseline. By the time I came down, she had called my father, told him I had finally crossed the line. She was turning me over to him. "Good luck," I heard her say as I came into the room. She hung up. "Your father will pick you up in ten minutes. Take this with you." She handed me the VCR tape, holding it between thumb and finger like roadkill. I went outside, sat on the porch steps and waited for Dad.

It didn't work out, of course. If I had pissed Mom off with a sex orgy, I really pissed my dad off by chewing with my mouth open. After a couple of weeks, I moved out of Dad's apartment and into Davie's basement. I went to school most of the time, but not to many of my classes. I don't know what I thought would happen. I skated every night and worked on my old Mustang in the auto shop during the day. Sometimes I sat around and gabbed with the shop teacher. Mr. Johnson was an old geezer, but not rich. I told him about my mom anyway, thinking how handy he would be as a stepfather, all those tools. He never called her, that I knew of anyway.

What did happen was that Mr. Edwards, my counselor, found me in the pit under my car and squatted down to tell me that my mother informed him that my life was my own. I was in charge. I could graduate or not. Whatever. She was handing me over to myself. He'd no longer be concerned either. He reached in and shook my oily hand. "See ya around," he said. I should have been happy with that news. Instead, I drank beer until I cried, got kicked out of Davie's basement, camped at Todd's.

I waited for another call to the counselor's office and it didn't come. And my friends evaporated, leaving me sleeping in Todd's backyard and eating leftovers after his mother went to work in the morning. "All you need is a grocery cart," Kenny commented one day, and maybe that's why I took a shower and walked into Mr. Edward's office and said I wanted to graduate. His "Good," made me lightheaded and after I sat down, we figured it all out. As some sort of peace offering, Mom threw a couple of Grishams on my bed to welcome me back home. Her only lecture that time was that I should not wear a baseball cap day and night, that it would make me bald, and I am living proof that she was right. The next year I started college in a state school that needed hockey players, and Sharon graduated and opened her business and met Wilfred. And Mom was on her own.

Like Sharon right now, maybe. I dialed her number again. Enid answered. "Hello. If you're calling for my father, his new number is 234-6908. The rest of us are still here." She did not explain a thing, just gave the facts.

"Enid. This is Uncle Sam. How're you doing?"

"Great. Will made the traveling squad. He gets to go to Canada. So does Mom. I have to stay here with Dad."

"Your father is there?"

"No, you know that. He's going to come over when Mom can't be here. To take care of me. Like on this hockey trip."

"Oh," I said. Sharon could have asked me. I would have taken care of Enid. "Is your mother there?" The line went silent as Enid handed the phone to her mother.

"Sharon, you only told him to leave last night. You have custodial rights all under control, including out-of-town hockey trips? How do you do it?" I did not mean it as a compliment. Nobody could be that organized.

"Don't start in, Sammy. The trip arrangements were pre-kicking out. I'm going to keep things normal here, hockey, school, bedtime rituals. We start the next Potter book tonight. Do you think it is too violent for a nine-year-old? A friend cautioned me, said someone dies. . ."

"Sharon, breathe. You're sounding as if a few meds might be helpful again.

"I started them yesterday. Takes a few days to kick in."

"In the meantime, let me bring a pizza over. You go for a walk, see a friend. Let me take on *The Order of the Phoenix*; I've been wanting to read it. You'd be doing me and yourself a favor." I hadn't planned on babysitting, but Sharon was sounding like a windup doll, clattering, waving her arms. About to tip over.

"I need to keep busy. I've started a casserole: lamb and beans. I'll whip up a salad. I'm not up to friends yet. Waiting for the Zoloft. Yes, come on over for dinner, after I go to yoga. I love you."

That last sentence got me even more worried. We didn't say that unless the situation was desperate. Sharon, my competent sister, was calling for help.

Again. This time she didn't need a private eye, only a brother.

Mrs. Jensen opened my file and looked at the scores on the test I had taken. A preference test, she explained. "We do best at what we like doing," she explained. Later, if necessary, I would take an achievement test. At this point, she probably had enough information to focus. "You are physical, like to keep moving, risk-taking at times, and independent. You dislike working for someone else, would like to be in charge. However, you wouldn't mind being on a team of some sort; you value the relationships in that sort of environment. You are inclined to pull back when criticized although you think of yourself as open to it." She looked at me. "I'm interested in the fact that you list reading as your #2 activity after skating. What do you read?"

"Lately?" I asked. "Cussler, Billy Collins, Anais Nin, Allende, . . .and other stuff." I didn't mention *The Pleasure Principle*.

"Widely. I am assuming you also write and spell and have computer skills."

She flipped through my file again. "A couple of years of college?"

"Yes." She also didn't need to know that my grades got me kicked off the hockey team, so there was no reason to keep paying tuition. "And a couple of years on semi-pro hockey team in the midwest." Then I lied, as usual. "When I realized I wouldn't make it into the pros, I quit and went to work at a couple of arenas. My last job was here at the Silver Skates."

"Where you were fired." She was poking at her computer now, frowning and making little snuffs like she didn't like what she was reading. Her printer started whirling and a piece of paper rolled out. "Here's a starting point," she said. "Not quite right, but it could be good experience. Night manager at the A & W out on Route l0. You'd be in charge from six until 2:00 a.m., with a couple of people working for you. And you'd be active, on your feet."

I was back to nachos again. "And the risk-taking part?"

"High possibility of robbery. That's why the last guy left."

I told her I'd think about it.

I still had time to get to the rink and skate with Mary and Jane, and I grabbed the next bus, slunk into a seat and closed my eyes. A & W. I didn't even know what A & W meant. Almost and Whatever? The story of my life.

They were waiting for me, paper cups of hot liquid calling itself coffee in front of them, the table lunging towards me in welcome. "Put a napkin or something under this leg," Mary said. I did before I sat at the chair next to her, tossing my skates under the table. Both women had their power leather jackets on, and Jane had fortified her blue eyes with wide frames connected to her blouse by a gold chain. Apparently we were not skating yet.

"Sam," Mary began in her matter-of fact way, "you seem like a dreamer. And we think we need you."

Jane smiled at me, hesitant. "At least we think we need you." She raised her cup, smelled its contents, put it down, her eyes large behind her glasses.

"We do." Mary took over. "I grew up in this neighborhood, as you know. It was a good place to be a kid: a grocery and a drug store nearby, sidewalks to skate on, trees, houses full of children. Our school was four blocks away and all the kids walked to it every day.

When the mall opened, everyone was excited at first. We had a pizza parlor, a furniture warehouse, even a small department store all within walking distance. Then cars began racing through our quiet streets. In a few years the little drugstore closed, and the grocery. The park became an off ramp for the new freeway. Most of the families moved and our old houses, once we had left, became rentals and started to fall apart. The school closed, and the sidewalks, lined with weeds and grass, led to nowhere. When the arena was built next to the mall, the yards we once played in were asphalted over, and haciendas and arches of fast food restaurants took the place of the old chestnut trees that had shaded us each summer."

Jane interrupted. "I used to come West on the train to visit my aunt every summer. That's when I first met Mary. My aunt's house turned into a gas station, then a tire place, now it offers quick lube jobs. I always wonder whatever happened to the pair of dirty underpants I buried under a lilac bush the day I didn't make it home in time. I walked around almost naked the whole afternoon. I kind of liked the breeze under my skirt."

Mary's agenda didn't include underwear. "So, now the Comstock neighborhood is a depressed, ugly huddle of blocks, inhabited by folks who can't afford to do more than make monthly payments to landlords whose idea of maintenance is an occasional attack on carpenter ants. Crumbling parking lots and neon signs are the front door to what had been a sturdy, graceful set of 1920's houses and families. The neighborhood is bounded by two freeways and the mall. Now," she tapped a finger on the table top, "this is good and it's bad. The mall offers a feasible draw for small businesses, and the freeways give terrific access to the downtown commercial district. The drawback is that these same freeways isolate us from adjacent neighborhoods, which in turn means that the neighborhood is a small, private paradise, waiting to happen."

Paradise? My block, my little garage house? The ragged streets, curbs encrusted with petrified dog shit and mats of Gulpy cups? The anemic trees whose broken nubs of limbs were just now setting out yet another pathetic fringe of buds? My neighbor's house, shades down, its door opening and closing at odd hours of the night, voices like spooks floating into the dark air? The empty lot next to mine, its Do NOT Dump sign askew under a pile of black bags? Paradise?

"You have to close your eyes." Jane did just that. "I can remember the white houses, the kick-the-can games in the street on hot summer evenings, parents sitting on steps, talking. The park had a wading pool and a teetertotter. We used to sit under the trees and share sandwiches with our boyfriends." She opened her eyes, grinned at her friend. "Remember, Mary?"

Mary didn't waver. "We don't have a park anymore, but we do have an ice rink. That's where you come in." She sat back and nodded at me as if I should understand.

"I don't get it."

Both Jane and Mary sighed, and Jane suggested we go out for lunch to talk more after we skate. She pulled her skates out of her bag. Whatever they had in mind would wait until we worked out.

We did not eat at the nearby Taco Shanty. We drove into town and the waiter at Le Bistro lingered nearby as we chose our lunches from a handwritten menu. The day's special, boeuf en daube, appealed to the women, so I ordered it too. I had no idea what it cost, nor the bottle of red wine which perched at our elbows. I assumed I would not be paying the bill. Mary tucked the receipt into her wallet when the meal ended. "Think it over," she said. "If you are in, get your plan on paper, say in a couple of weeks?"

Instead of shaking my hand, as Mary had, Jane hugged me, said, "I hope you'll do it." Mary was the brains, and Jane the heart of this scheme. Both apparently had deep pockets and friends in high places. My role? Maybe they just needed a good-looking young guy around.

That was my little interior joke as I walked home. You're showing your hubris again, Mom would have warned. So I tried to be rational. Two wealthy women have decided to rehabilitate a whole neighborhood, including its houses, its empty lots, and possibly its inhabitants. They believe that a neighborhood needs safe streets and growing families. It needs access to the outside, but not the traffic such access often encourages. It needs common goals and pride and green lawns. And a neighborhood needs a center, a place for people to gather. Their old neighborhood, Comstock, fits their criteria, nestled next to a freeway off ramp, bounded by a mall and a series of streets leading to nowhere, filled with dilapidated housing stock and empty buildable lots. And this is where I come in, an ice arena that will be the living room of the community. That's what Jane called it, a living room. Thinking about it had me talking to myself again.

That's why I could have said yes even before the hug.

The women had already pulled together the board of corporate representatives which would join them in the rehab of the houses. Their realtors were visiting landlords with money in hand. Their contractors were estimating costs on individual houses. Their team of public relations experts were scheduling a series of meetings with homeowners to explain the plan, to offer low interest loans if they wished to become partners in the renovation. They had met with the city to discuss improvements to the streets, plantings along the off ramp and on the parkways and the possibilities of affordable housing funds for new construction. The project would take at least five years. My part in it would be coordinating the transformation of the ice arena into a living room.

By the time I got home, I could hardly breathe. Not from excitement. From second thoughts. How could I imagine that I could manage anything? I could hardly manage my life. Mary called me a dreamer, that's why they asked me to join them. But when had any of my dreams ever worked out? The only real dream in my life had been to play pro hockey, which ended in Des Moines, Iowa, in the midst of a storm of boos. My other dream was not really a dream but a hope, and it took me only two years to fuck up that one.

I was afraid to dream again.

Then I thought of A & W. No risky dream there, handing out tin roof sundaes and instructing workers how to clean out the deep fryer. It wouldn't be so bad--no pressure and all I could eat. All day to write or read. Maybe, on my off hours, I could teach skating to little kids who would grow up dreaming about being hockey players. As Mom would say, what goes round comes round.

Then I couldn't stand thinking any more. I called Rose, but her phone was turned off so I headed over to Sharon's and the lamb and beans. Perhaps Harry Potter would help.

CHAPTER FIFTEEN

I had forgotten Sharon's recent state of mind until I walked through the door. Something was burning, the lamb, I guessed. "Mommy, Mommy!" greeted me from the kitchen. Smoke trailed out of the vents above the oven, Enid stood on a stool and leaned into the haze. "I think it's on fire!" she yelled and when she saw me, she leaped into my arms. "Help!"

I put her down and looked through the oven window. Red tongues flickered behind the glass; the oven looked like a little fireplace. I couldn't remember what Mom used to pour on oven fires, in her case usually involving ignited berry pie juice. Not water. Salt? Flour? Salt, I guessed, and I grabbed the round container from the cupboard and opened the oven door. Oh, I recalled too late. Turn off the oven and be careful opening the door. All that oxygen. I poured salt over what I thought was the site of the flames, my fingers tingling and hairless if I could judge by the new smell in the air. I flung the door shut again. Enid's scream sirened through the house, and I heard a door slam, someone pounding down the stairs. Will's stockinged feet slid to a hockey stop in front of the oven.

"Oh, oh," he said. "Mom said to keep an eye on it in case it overflowed. I guess it did." The fire had burnt itself out, and salt smoldered under the dripping pot.

The kid had enough troubles. "Open a window!" I commanded, "and bring a spatula and some rags." I opened the oven door. "And some hot pads or something. We're going to clean up this mess." The casserole lid was stuck and I couldn't see what had happened inside, so we spent a few minutes scraping the salt and crud from the oven floor. Then I pried the pot open and found sweet-smelling lamb and beans. We wiped off the pot's outside, poured off a little juice, replaced it in the scraped-off oven and turned the heat on to low. Then I gave Will a high five and told Enid to zipper her lips if she wanted Harry Potter anytime in the next five years. I loved the way she ran her finger over her mouth, her eyes so solemn and trustworthy.

Which meant, of course, that the minute Sharon came home from yoga, her daughter made her bend over to hear a whispered secret. Sharon looked at me, her eyes wide, but then her face went still, a remnant of the yoga maybe, and she whispered back, "It's okay," to Enid, who wouldn't look at me. She sent the kids to the playroom and poured herself a glass of water.

"It's dehydrating,," she explained. "The yoga." She sat down at the table and closed her eyes. "I can do it in the middle of the floor now, head stand. Shows I can still learn."

"That's good, middle of the floor." The kids were quiet, the kitchen fragrant with casserole perfume, perfect for my sermon, the one about ghosts pointing our way, about the need to accept them, let them settle into nooks and crannies.

"Yes it is. You feel very strong and very alone standing on your head. I think I can do this." She didn't mean yoga. "I'm giddy with excitement one moment and drowning in sadness the next. Headstand was one of the few times today, except for right now, when my keel was even. I don't know what will happen, and right now, with you here, my children nearby, it doesn't matter. I have a sense that as long as I have these calm moments, I'll manage to get through the chaotic ones."

She got up and poured a glass of wine, looked at me and took out a beer when I nodded. The burst of words I had practiced a day or so before dissipated into a faint whiff of casserole smoke lingering in the corners of the room. My profound insight into ghosts and their care was not intended for Sharon. She had her own ways of understanding what was happening to her. Those ghosts were mine to manage.

"I like Rose," Sharon said, as she handed me the bottle. "She's real." She paused, "Do you like her?"

I could have said, "She's okay," like I used to when Sharon asked me the same question about my high school loves. I probably even said it when she asked about Reba. Maybe I didn't want to admit to the feelings I was having at those times, that somehow those feelings endangered me or changed me. This time I said, "Yes. I do. A lot." And I didn't crumble, explode, or become a gaseous fume. Instead, I grinned, made a little noise in my throat, grinned again.

At first, Sharon smiled back, and then she bit her upper lip and gave a little moan. "My brother is growing up," she said with no trace of sisterly sarcasm. If growing up for Sharon meant standing on her head, alone and strong, it seemed that for me it meant allowing myself to become putty in somebody's arms. At the moment the arms were my sister's.

"I wish Mom were here," she said. "Guess I'll have to do, okay?." She let me go and started to get up.

I told her to wait a minute. The smoke and flames of a near disaster needed to be dealt with. "I have a little of Mom in me, too," I said. "Including the need to lecture. Like, should a little kid be in charge of a casserole?"

Sharon shook her head. "I'm still a little wobbly, Sam. Sometimes, in head stand, it helps to have someone you trust faintly touch the back of your leg, to let you know when it's veering away from its true path to the ceiling. You're getting good at that."

A person had to learn to trust a moment like that. I looked at my beautiful sister and knew that when I stood and reached for another beer, the moment would be gone, lost in a clutter of chairs scraping, children calling, tomorrow intruding. So I didn't move, tried to incise it somewhere inside me to run my fingers over when I needed it.

We ate the casserole, and I read the first couple of chapters of Harry. Then the kids headed off to bed and I reached for my jacket.

Sharon wasn't quite finished. "I told you to think about Mom's last story, Sam. Have you?"

I wanted to protest, tell her I had really important things on my mind, like my future, a couple of old rich ladies, and so on, but something about the quaver in her voice stopped me. "Not much."

"Well, I have. What if Mom was trying to tell us that while we may have lived an entire life with someone, or not, we have children, or not, we achieve success of some sort, or not, when it comes to the end, it is the fragile thread of love that has unwound and snagged against our days that we cling to, give over to, finally, like Frank holding his daughter's hand, as he listens to Edie's voice over his shoulder."

I could imagine that.

"Not somebody else's love for us," she went on. "Our love for somebody else."

I thought about it for a minute. I could imagine that thread winding its way through my life, knotted in places, thin at times, steady, like right now as I sat next to my sister. "I like that idea," I said. "So would Mom." I kissed her on the cheek as I left.

Rose still wasn't answering her phone. I had decided sometime during the evening not to unload on Sharon the proposition about the ice rink. One, I didn't want to interrupt what was happening between us, and two, my sister had always thought I was prone to weirdness. She might have believed that renovating an entire decrepit neighborhood was the latest in a string of ill-advised brotherly pipe dreams, including the hockey career and the marriage. She might also have reminded me that a year or two ago, I invested my savings, such as they were, in a $5000 movie, and my money had been drunk up over two weekends of shoots and the rental of a stedi-cam by a crew whose expertise extended only an inch or two beyond point-and-shoot. *Savage Virgin* existed in title only, the entire footage on the editing room. At least that's what my friend, the producer, claimed, furious that his first film didn't even make it to DVD.

"Learn from your mistakes," Mom would have said. "Look before you leap." I had made a career of failing to learn that lesson. In this case, what I needed was someone to advise me about politics and real estate investment and how to go about a renovation of an ice rink. Someone full of integrity, whose viewpoint was untarnished by self-interest. Someone who owed me. My father.

I had not talked to him since before Mom died. A year ago, he had offended me by asking when I would start doing something with my life after I had hinted, in the early days of my unemployment, that a loan would be much appreciated. I wondered, as I dialed his home number, if he would remember my asshole comment. Perhaps he had hung up before I said it. Dad didn't come to Mom's memorial service, but Sharon said he always sent the kids gifts on their birthdays, calling to make sure they arrived. Everything was fine with him and Janelle, he always said when Sharon asked. Cheerful and younger than Dad, Janelle had been shoes-off strict about the carpets in their new house, overly mindful of her step children's eating habits, but an okay person to visit once in a while. We never stayed overnight because they had only one small guest room. When Sharon went off to college and I just went off, the only real contact I had with Janelle was the week or so I tried to live in their house.

After that, my father and I would meet once in a while for lunch, and I began to understand that Dad and I lived on separate planets, except for hockey. He came to my in-town games and I liked hearing him yell at me and the referee whenever I was on the ice, just like the other dads.

My wedding was the first time my whole family stood in the same room in ten years. Everybody smiled, including Mom, who made a point of walking up to Janelle and giving her a little familial hug. This impressed my in-laws and for a while, at least, they seemed reassured that their daughter had married into a civilized group of people.

My fingers jittered over the buttons on the phone. If I stopped, I'd never try this again. The phone rang, rang, finally, "Hello." Not a message recorder. Janelle.

"Hi. This is Sam." I should have asked about her, made some sort of conversation after all this time. Instead, "Is my dad home?"

"Sam!" I could see her red lips broadening into a smile. "How are you?"

"Good. I need to talk to Dad if he's around."

"He's right here." I could hear her hand wrap around the mouthpiece. A moment later, "Hello, Sam."

I had not prepared for the sound of his voice, tight, a note or two higher than I remembered, as if he were having trouble speaking. Perhaps he was. I was. "I would like to talk to you about something, a proposition that involves a rink and a lot of real estate. I . . ." the words stuck, then spurted out, "I need your advice." I waited.

My father cleared his throat. "You want me to go in on a scheme of some sort? You should know by now I don't invest that way." His evening beard scratched against the phone, buzzed at me.

It was my turn to clear my throat. "No money. Just advice. Unless you don't want to. I can find somebody else." I tried to chuckle, added, "I don't blame you for wondering what I'm up to, and I'll warn you, it may end up being absolutely nothing." I almost hung up. So stupid.

"How about lunch tomorrow? You can tell me about it over a turkey sandwich at Hurley's. 11:30, Okay?"

Hurley's was the restaurant we used to go to when we were father and son, out for a Saturday lunch after a morning hockey game. "See you there," I answered, hoping I didn't sound too eager.

Mary asked for a plan. Dad, knowing me, would not expect that I'd have one. I sat down at the iMac and added a new folder to its desktop. It wasn't like I had decided to take Mary and Jane up on their offer. I just wanted to think about it a little while. I called the folder "The Living Room."

At first I just wrote down whatever came to mind: smelly rubber mats, tongue-blackening coffee, windows, bathrooms, skates and managers who had outlived their purposes. I got it all out of my system. Then I thought about what the building could be, how the ice would be the center of the activities, but the other things that could happen there, like childcare, family nights, after school activities, a video lending library, a quiet place to read the newspaper over a good cup of coffee, crafts classes, a social services office for the elderly, shit, maybe even a neighborhood employment agency. The building had a second floor above the sheet of ice. The lot was big enough for another sheet or maybe an indoor soccer and basketball gym. Maybe a swimming pool, or even better, a little park with a wading pool.

My list exploded into three pages of jagged notes. A couple of hours later, exhausted, I reread them and I knew they were good ideas, really good. But then I leaned back and took a deep breath, and a shudder of reality swept through me, landed like lead in the pit of my stomach. I looked at the pages again. All I saw was words, a bunch of them, flung out like a gloveful of ice chips. If they lay there a minute or two, they'd disappear into the smooth surface beneath them. As usual, I had no plan. I didn't know what a plan was.

I was into my fourth beer when I finished my latest Stephen King. I tried a poem or two from Billy Collins, but he had things way too figured out. I needed to get out of my head. Isabel Allende was too far out of my head. I needed something that would not make me work, just go with whatever flow I still had in me. I pulled a thin book from the shelf, read the first sentence, "He was an old man who fished alone in a skiff in the Gulf Stream and he had gone eighty-four days without taking a fish." Hemingway. Mom had lent it to me when I was fourteen and I remembered skimming pages, looking for the excitement, hating the end. I yelled at her through her open bedroom door, "I don't get it. The guy hung on for days and all he got was a pile of bones." I flung the book at the hump of her knees.

"You will, someday," she said. "I'll save it for you." She picked it up, pressed a bent page, and closed it. She smiled. "You'll see."

Page 39 still had a crease in it. Hello, again, it whispered. Maybe this would be the day. I lay down on my sofa and began.

When the phone rang, I couldn't answer it because I was crying. For no good reason. Real chokes and sobs, no blinking and swallowing. I wiped by eyes on my T-shirt and tried to focus. I wouldn't have been surprised to find that my tears had left blue or green or red stains on my sleeve. My inner crannies felt raw and empty. I breathed and my lungs ached when the cool air hit them. Finally I picked up the phone.

"I'm calling at a bad time?" Rose asked.

"I have just met the old man and the sea, and I'll never feel sorry for myself again." I meant it just then, a gasp of a hiccup warning me not to explain. "Actually, I'm kind of a mess. You probably don't want to talk to me right now."

I suppose I sounded suicidal, because Rose said she'd be right over. She hung up before I could explain that I could tell the difference between a book and real life, not to worry.

Rose took one look at me and my coffee table trunk and started picking up bottles and papers. "Bad day?" she asked. I pointed at Hemingway.

"I read this once," she said. " *Old Man and the Sea.* It's an allegory of the human spirit, isn't it? Hemingway thought it was his best book." She flipped through the pages. "Can I borrow it?"

"I have a big dead skeleton on my hook, too," I answered. "No allegory. The real thing."

Rose was in the kitchen, cleaning out the sink. "You need a couple cups of coffee, Sam." She measured the grounds, started the pot, checked the fridge. "and some food. When did you eat last?"

She finally sat down next to me, "Skeleton?"

I pointed at the papers piled on the table and told her about Mary and Jane, their offer. "I tried to make a plan. I really liked thinking about the possibilities, but when I finished and read what I had written, I knew that I was doing it again, like always. Dreaming. Nothing could possibly come of this pile of shit."

The thing about Rose was that she didn't try to talk me out of it. She just nodded and sipped her coffee, her eyes kind and accepting.

"The old man dreamed and he hung onto his dream until it was worthless.

What good did it do him? In the end, he had nothing anyway. Did he?"

Rose shrugged.

"Well, did he? I mean, there's no way I'm going to convince somebody to spend a couple of million dollars just because I want them to. Me, an unemployed jerk who's never gotten his shit together his entire life."

"Santiago wasn't an unemployed jerk. The analogy doesn't work."

"You know what I mean. This whole thing is like going fishing and maybe catching something you can't possibly land and then really fucking up."

"Besides his dream, Santiago had a boat, a pole and bait."

"That too. I'm not equipped for this expedition."

"Stop thinking of this damned list as a fish skeleton. It's the bait, don't you see? And you need to find the rest of the stuff." She stood up, reached for her coat. "You aren't even half ready to dream." She picked up the book and opened it. 'Man is not made for defeat. . .A man can be destroyed but not defeated.' This is not a sad book, Sam. It's an instruction book on how to be human."

The other thing about Rose was that she stayed very calm when she was very angry, so calm I didn't know how angry she was until the door slammed and her black boots stomped down my porch stairs and into the night.

I picked up my list. As bait, it might work. What I needed was a boat and a pole. An organized plan and a way of presenting it. That's what I'd say when I met Dad for lunch. In the meantime, I needed to find my iron and press a pair of pants and a shirt. And somewhere in a drawer I still had the necktie Mom gave me as a going-away present the second or third time I set off from her house to make my way in the world. If I kept busy I wouldn't think about what that skeleton really meant.

"You don't mean Mary Perry, do you?" Hurley's was an old men's club turned public, walnut paneling and carpet. Dad's question bounced off its dark walls and sank into the plush floor under our table. Other conversations were going on around us, but only murmurs flowed past, a good place to talk business, I supposed.

"Yeh, Mary Perry, older woman, still looks good."

"She should. She is one of the wealthiest women in town. Her husband was in lumber, actually, three generations of the Perrys were, and he sold out when the sources started drying up. And the other woman?"

"Jane Mason. She's divorced, I think, about the same age as Mary, maybe sixty?'

"She got a tidy piece of Intel when she divorced the second time. The first husband gave her the house and a monthly income which I hear is more than most folks make in a year. She knows how to pick ex-husbands." Dad laughed, then looked at the menu, apparently not willing to continue on that particular topic. "What'll you have?"

He needn't have asked. I always had the hot turkey sandwich at Hurley's. Just thinking about the mashed potatoes and gravy took me back fifteen years. 'How's Janelle?" I asked after the waiter had taken our orders.

"She's busy with her volunteer work, playing tennis, and she's getting into fused glass. She's always on the go. She said to say hello."

She would. She was thoughtful that way. "And you're busy, too, I guess."

Dad sighed, said he had thought of retiring but the business had picked up lately. He'd had to hire another guy, and he was traveling a lot. "The consulting business has revived," he said, "now that the economy has." My father had built his company from scratch, once he left a management job in local government. He specialized in helping private groups and public groups work together on projects.

He greased the gears, he used to say. The last I'd heard he was making $250 an hour greasing. I hoped that since I was his son, he'd do it for the price of a lunch, the cash for which I had in my back pocket.

The plates came. The turkey still smelled as good as it used to be. Dad thought so too, because he took a bite and said, "Just like old times, almost," and I nodded, thinking of my dead mother. I guessed that's what the "almost" meant, for he went on, "I didn't come to your mother's service because I didn't want to make anyone uncomfortable. Janelle told me I should have."

I shrugged. What could I say, that we didn't even miss him?

Dad pushed his plate away. "What do you want to talk about, Sam?"

Something about the question, the fatherliness of it, made me look away, think for a second of all of the questions I had stored up for him, all beginning with Why?

But I caught him glancing at his watch. This was not the time and perhaps there would never be a time. I leaned over and pulled up the plastic folder I had stored under my chair. "Living Room."

After Rose left, I had spent most of the night reorganizing my list under categories like: Programs, Mechanics, Renovation, New Construction, Future Expansions. The waiter refilled my empty water glass several times, and I kept talking until I ran out of words.

Then Dad start talking, adding more headings: Community Input, Government Support/coordination, Cost estimates, Architectural and Engineering. He gave me the names of several activists interested in urban renewal and said he'd give a friend a call in the urban design department at the university. He pulled out his old Palmpilot and jotted a reminder to send me several model proposals of similar projects from other towns, and when he looked up at me, I saw him as he appeared to others, bright eyes, fit and energetic, his veined slender hands moving in enthusiastic swoops as he talked. He was working hard to convince me to believe in my own idea. If I had been wearing ice skates, he would have been on his knees, pulling the skate hook, tightening the strings, looking up and saying, "You can do it, Sam."

But now, he looked at his watch again and said, “Oh, oh.” Then, “Sam, run with this. It’s good. You’ve got several very able investors, and an exciting plan.“ As he reached for his wallet to pay the bill, I told him I’d get it and he laughed. “A first time for everything.” He seemed pleased as he looked back, waved, and threaded his way between the tables. “I’ll call you,” he called as he hurried out the door.

If the plan was the bait, Dad would be the boat, leaving me as the pole. My job was to stick my neck out over the water and be patient.

“You forgot Santiago,” Rose reminded me when she finally answered her phone and I could tell her about lunch. “Who’s the fisherman?” Maybe Mary and Jane? Or maybe allegories don’t work in real life. Maybe a person has to learn how to be human and vulnerable and full of hope first hand. Maybe that’s what Hemingway was saying all along.

CHAPTER SIXTEEN

Three weeks later, I had the preliminary plan almost finished. The first step was to buy a couple of shirts, a jacket, and two ties, which I charged to my Visa. On the way home with my packages, I looked down at my Adidas and went back into the mall for a pair of leather shoes. And dark socks, not white. Then I began meeting with everyone we could find who could be helpful in getting the new arena and meeting place, the Comstock Living Room, rolling. I talked to city people, architects, and foundations who might be persuaded to grant funds. I met with consessioneers, equipment suppliers, and even the county librarian who was eager to install a branch library in the new building. Then, I visited Lee Chin and asked him how much he was asking for the arena.

He pretended he didn't know what I was talking about. "I do not want to sell," he said, but his drumming fingers on the top of his desk indicated something different.

"Too bad," I said and got up. "I had heard otherwise and I might have had a buyer." I picked up my new almost-leather briefcase and headed for the door. Of course, he called me back and we talked some more. I pointed out the decrepit condition of the lobby, the age of the ice-making equipment and the rusting Zamboni, among other things. When we finished talking a week later, over too many cups of bad coffee, since we met at the arena instead of his downtown office, we almost had a deal.

That is, the company almost had a deal. Mary and Jane had become a not-for-profit corporation, Perry/Mason, Inc. I was a hired hand, the arena project manager, and got my first paycheck the week my unemployment ran out. I also got a company car, a conscientious Prius. I stopped the unemployment office to tell Mrs. Jensen my news.

"I actually didn't think the A&W was for you," she said. "Congratulations, and, ah, good luck." I had a feeling she was not sure about this job, either.

I liked the busy-ness, the hand shakes, even the new shoes. I went to bed at night smoldering with ideas, woke up reaching for my iphone, a gift from Dad.

The problem was, of course, that Rose and I barely saw each other. We talked late at night on the phone, tried and gave up on phone sex, both our heads full of our days. She had finished her second draft of her novel, decided to keep the fatal disease, calling the book "Mom" for now, and was pitching it to a couple of local agents. They seemed interested and had asked for the first hundred pages, so she had begun the third edit. "It's hardest of all. I'm killing my babies," she moaned. Even in that sad state, she was a good listener and I told her about meeting the mayor, talking with the city planning director, and my daily meetings with my two skating partners. None of us had had a pair of skates on since all this started.

"You should. Get back to your roots, which reminds me," Rose said, "I'm going black again. It'll look great on the book cover." If I had been as good a listener as she, I would have warned her to remember Santiago and the marlin, and not go so far out into the sea.

When we talked a long week later, her voice was as dark as I imagined her hair to be. "They each sent it back. 'Not my kind of book,' one of the agents wrote on the form rejection slip. The other one actually typed a little note: 'To represent a book, I simply have to fall in love with it. That didn't happen with MOM. Sorry."

"You sound kind of destroyed, Rose. I don't blame you." The world according to Hemingway. "But you finished a novel, you continue to work on it and it's work you love, and you tell a story rich with truth and humor. You might be destroyed, at this moment, but you aren't defeated. At least, I can't imagine it."

"Oh, fuck off," she answered and hung up. Damn, I might be

getting my public life a little more in order, I thought, as I redialed her number, but my private life was going to hell. She didn't answer.

The other person who fell between the cracks those weeks was my sister. After I told her about the project, the fact that Mary and Jane wanted to use me in their project and how I wanted to be used by them, Sharon said, "You're going to be busy. I don't want to bother you, so just call me once in a while? Or come by?" And I did a couple of times. As far as I could tell, everything was going okay at her house. Sharon had found a Laotian woman to babysit when she was at yoga or at her counselor's, and one time I walked in to find Wilfred reading Harry Potter to the kids and all of them laughing. "Ugh!" Enid yelled. "Ron's throwing up slugs. Want to listen, Uncle Sam?" I begged off and left. Why did I feel sad at the sight of a father and his children laughing together? One, because I knew it didn't happen every evening; and two, a month earlier, I believed I would be reading those pages to my nephew and niece. And three. It felt a little like I'd lost my family. But just then my cell phone vibrated.

I was shaving for the second time that day. I had a dinner meeting with a foundation chair and his committee at which I would introduce the idea of a living room for a reviving neighborhood, a place to come together, no, too much of a cliche', a place where neighbors could, what? . . .The phone rang.

"Sam?" Sharon sounded as if she didn't recognize my voice.

"Hi," I answered, swiping my chin and the phone with a spritz of aftershave. "What's up?"

"Can you come over tonight? I've found something in Mom's things I don't understand. Her ring, remember? The little ruby? I was cleaning out my jewelry box and. . . ."

I interrupted her. "I'm out the door, Sis." Then I regretted my hurried words, my aftershave, my "Sis." When had I ever called her that? "I'm sorry. I'm running late. How about tomorrow?" I skimmed through my schedule and found an hour. "How about a late lunch? At l:30?" I had a lunch date at 11:30. I could pretend to be hungry two hours later.

"Here. At l:30. Don't forget, Sam." Her warning made me think that I'd probably forgotten some other date lately, like I had fallen into a forgetting mode where she was concerned.

"Won't," I assured her, buttoning the shirt I had bought that afternoon. I probably should have ironed out the new shirt creases, but I didn't have time.

The next day, Sharon was waiting for me at the door when I drove up. Daffodils and tulips glowed red and pink and yellow on the terrace, and a salad and a glass of wine, Sharon's half-empty, waited at each place at the table. I sat down and felt the sun on my skin "God, this feels good," I said. When did spring happen?

Sharon said eat, the salad's wilting, as she fumbled a small box out of her pocket. "This is what I want to talk to you about, Sam." She opened it. Inside a red stone shimmered in the bright light.

"Mom's." I recognized it from the day we cleaned out her house.

"Look at it," Sharon said.

The gold band was wide, the stone set within the embrace of a smooth gold mound, a breast of gold, a ruby nipple. I pulled the ring over the tip of my index finger. "Weird," I said.

"Look at the inscription."

I turned the ring over, squinted until I could read: "Forever, Adrienne."

"Who's Adrienne?" I asked.

"You don't get it, do you?" Sharon grabbed the ring from my hand, held it up as if I should be receiving a message. "Adrienne. A woman!" She gave me her "you jerk" look and then emptied her glass of wine. "Woman," she repeated as if I should disintegrate at the sound of the word.

"So?" I tried to calm her with a disinterested half-smile. I was not going to be pulled into my sister's frenzy again. "So she had a friend. So?"

"So!" she yelled. Then she took a breath and asked. "What word did you have engraved on the underside of Reba's ring?"

"Forever," I remembered.

"And I have a 'Forever' pressing into my almost-divorced third finger. Everybody says, 'Forever.' Every lover, even lesbian lovers, even our mother's lover. "

We sat blinking at each other under the yellow sun. "But wait," I finally said. "What about the guy with the gut, the other one she went out with?"

"Decoys."

"No, wait, Sharon. Think about that story, the one called 'First Time?'"

"I have thought about it. Adrien, his name was. Change the pronouns and it could have been Adrienne and Mom. And maybe a dildo. Could have happened any time. Before the divorce, during, after, as long as her lover had thick glasses."

I reached into my pocket and pulled out my vibrating phone.

Sharon stood and picked up our plates. "Go on your way, Sam, and do the stuff you have to do right now. Let's talk when you have more time." She looked over her shoulder. "And yes, the kids and I are doing fine."

"Sam, here," I answered my phone.

Sharon was pissed and rightly so, I thought as I drove away. I just couldn't deal with her situation right then. I certainly didn't want to think about Mom. What good did it do? She had lived her life and now she was gone. No matter how many Adriennes we found hidden in her jewelry box, it just didn't matter anymore.

The thing about being a successful was that it was not a 100% deal. Perry/Mason Inc. thought of me as their golden boy, and so far, I could do no wrong. We already had two grants in place, a city council ready to vote in rehab and low income housing funds, and I had gotten a promise from Wayne Gretzke to come to our first event in the rehabbed arena. The library's architect was working with the group we commissioned to design the new addition, and I had a Zamboni on order.

However, my relationship with the now black-haired Rose, sucked. She had taken a workshop on marketing her novel and was spending her days writing synopses and sending out queries to agents all over the country and getting the usual rejections. When I called, which was not as often as her despair demanded, she often hung up after a couple of exchanges. Our weekends deteriorated into a couple of hours of pizza and TV, and listless thrustings on the sofa or futon that left us both exhausted, she wet-eyed and depressed.

"I can't stand what is happening to you, Sam," she said one night as she wrapped herself in her cape and pushed her feet into her shoes. "All you talk about is yourself and your goddammed arena. I'm sick of it." She opened the door. "Whatever happened to the guy who read poetry? Or Jack? Have you abandoned Jack too?" The door slammed before I could think of what to answer. Then I got mad. Jack, for godsakes. For once in my life I was making something of myself and she should support me, not cut me down. I followed her out the door, caught up with her, grabbed her.

"You're not being fair," I said, the words coming out of the pissed twelve-year-old kid who had taken over.

"Fuck you," Rose answered as she jerked her arm back from my fingers. Then she turned and ran away. I watched, barefooted and freezing in my boxers, until she turned a corner, whatever I was making of myself not clear even to me.

The next day Sharon showed me the ring, that afternoon Dad and I met for what had become a weekly debriefing session on the project. He had been hired as one of the consultants, and when I left his office, I realized I didn't think of him as a prick any longer, more like a smart person with high standards. I believed that his opinion of me was going through the same kind of morphing.

I decided to walk over to Rose's apartment and do some repair work on our rocky road. I stuck a bottle of merlot in my raincoat pocket to help smooth the way . From my house, I had to pass by Coffee Tyme, and I walked in, thinking that I could start the evening with lattes to go. The place jangled, and even though half the crowd was staring at chess boards, an electric jazz guitar warbled over their heads. I looked around. At a back table I found Rose's black head, resting against a dreadlocked-padded shoulder, both shaking with laughter. Malcolm's two-fingered hand mushed into her hair, and after a moment or two, it moved across her clean white chin.

"Lattes?"

I took the cups outside where I dumped them in the drain at the street corner. Then I went home to find thirteen new e-mail messages on my Perry/Mason-provided P.C. In less than a day, I had managed to piss off the only two people I really cared about. I set the wine on the drainboard and found a beer in the fridge.

Mom's iMac signaled with its undulating orange eye from the corner of the desk where I had shoved it. I yelled, "What?" It didn't answer, of course, but I kept talking. "You're here for no good reason. You tell me three stories and so what? They don't mean anything. You want me to write? I'm no writer. For once, you're wrong, Mom. I'm a doer. I've always been a doer. I fucked up a few times, but I'm not fucking up now. I'm doing. You, above all people, should be happy for me. " Damn, I felt like crying again. I pushed the button and the iMac started breathing. The three folders appeared: Jack's and Mom's stories, my Living Room plan. I had to stop feeling sorry for myself, get my mind off the look on Sharon's face, the fingers in Rose's hair, the loneliness of this room.

I opened Jack's folder. He had said Namaste to Vicki, his former wife, and walked away to wherever. I recalled identifying with Jack a little too closely at that moment and switching off the computer. Later, Jack visits the black-haired girl and has great sex and then gets jealous and was kicked out of her life. I knew what was going to happen to him next. He was going to design a skateboard park, become an expert, travel and get rich. And he would wonder, every once in a while, as he sat in his far-flung hotel rooms late at night, whatever happened to the black-haired girl with the diamond in her nose.

I tried calling her, but she wasn't answering. I opened the bottle of merlot.

Sharon didn't answer either when I called the next morning. I had awakened with one of those headaches that start inside your nose, bore through your brain and settle in the back of your neck. Red wine, again. By ten I had taken four aspirins and I could think ahead enough to cancel a couple of appointments. By eleven, after a stomach-seizure at the toilet bowl and a rest on the tiles, I came to the conclusion that I was becoming my former father, a prick, like the one his children didn't care much for, the one who came home in time to kiss them goodnight, whose sign of affection was to rub a scratchy beard on tired cheeks, who spent weekends at his desk writing on yellow-lined paper. The father, I had to remind myself, who didn't miss a hockey game. Not all bad, but lonely, I bet. Lonely enough to find a pretty red-lipped woman who made him feel whole.

Like Frank. Perhaps my mother's story was an exercise in imagining the what-ifs: what if, despite the red-lipped woman, Mom and Dad had stayed married? What if they had grown old, deaf, ditzy, and blind together? What if a child came forward to rescue them, to relieve them of the catastrophe of age? What if the red-lipped woman lived on only in the secret parts of the aging man? Choices. Not a matter of right and wrong, but choices made in the real time of the moment, lives following behind. My mother was a good guesser. I knew Frank and Edie more intimately than I knew either of my parents.

Four more aspirins and I was able to think about getting out of the house and going for a walk. In the couple of hours I had spent on my sofa, I had developed a new vision of my life, triangular in shape. One angle, not necessarily the first angle, held my job. The second angle contained my family, my sister, my father. An elusive, but compelling woman, Rose, occupied the third angle . At the moment the triangle was equilateral, but the angles could expand, decrease, depending on the day, the moment, the urgency.

180 degrees divided into three essential parts. I was in charge the size of each part. If I didn't take charge, as I hadn't in the past month or so, my life would become a straight line. And I would end

up walking down a sidewalk, like I was now, towards Rose's flower stand behind which a stranger stood.

"Rose?" I asked.

"She's gone." At least, that's what I heard.

"Gone?"

"Home. To the East Coast." Seeing my face, he added, "For a couple of weeks. Her mom was sick or something."

I put down the bunch of violets I had thought of handing through a narrowly opened door, a sign of repentance or hope or something. "Don't suppose you know exactly where?"

"Nope." He looked at me and I must have appeared pathetic enough to make him add, "Sheila might, though." He handed me a card. "She owns the business."

I put the card in my pocket and headed for Shaker's. Davie was there, as usual, standing at the bar arguing with someone and pointing at the TV screen. "Hey!" I said as I settled next to him on a stool.

"Where you been?" Davie scowled and his eyes flickered towards the screen. "You missed everything."

Where the hell were Jake and Todd and Barney? It was the last week of March madness. They had to be dead. I signaled for a Bud. "Like what?"

Davie finally looked at me. "We waited for you to come in but we figured you had gone away or something. Barney got married a couple of weeks ago, kind of quick, and we wanted to have a party when they came back from the judge. We thought of your house, but since you weren't around, and my wife didn't want to traumatize the kids, we went to Jake's new apartment." Davie's voice lowered as he leaned into my closest ear. "We were doing some stuff and had a keg. A lot of people showed up uninvited and it got kind of rough. The neighbors called the cops. When it all finally settled down, only the people too scared or too juiced to jump off the balcony or run down the fire escape were left, holding the baggies, so to speak. That happened to be Todd and Jake. Barney and his bride hid in the janitor's closet."

"This group does wedding nights **real** well," I said. "So, where is everyone?"

"On probation. In Barney's case, lifetime housewife arrest." Davie turned his attention to the frenzied movement overhead. "Too bad. You really missed something." He shook his head and seemed to forget I was sitting beside him until the referee's whistle. "Damn!" he yelled. "Did you see that? That call cost me fifty bucks. Shit!"

Did this use to be fun? I tossed five bucks on the counter and left. I don't think Davie knew I left. Or cared.

If I ever imagined that I might need to build a fourth angle on my triangle, I could give up that thought. Friends weren't included in my geometric configuration; in fact, the whole idea was stupid and I had fucked off a whole day. The phone number on the card the kid gave me was disconnected, of course.

I stuck my cell phone in my coat pocket and walked the mile or so to Coffee Thyme and sank down on a chair under the heated awning. What the hell, venti triple. I needed a jolt. When it came, I closed my eyes and sucked it up. Then I felt a hand on my shoulder. "Game?" I opened my eyes to Malcolm and to the painted board in front of me.

"Malcolm," I said. "Go to hell."

He sat down across from me and in his two-fingered way, placed his cup next to mine. "Okay," he said.

Under the matted wads of hair, his eyes were blue, smiling. I could almost see him. "Sorry."

"Okay," he said.

For some reason it seemed important to know right then."How did you lose them? Your fingers?"

"Corn harvester. I tried to unclog it. Dumb mistake. The engine was still running."

I felt a swoop of relief. No gulf war, Afghanistan, no heroic feat. Just a stupidass mistake. "Oh," I answered. "Must have hurt."

"Changed my life. One mindless moment, and I'm a writer and not an Eastern Oregon grain farmer like my father and his father."

He held up his arm and I could see a tatooed vine, its bright green leaves disappearing into his shirt sleeves. "I'm reconnected, more-or-less. They saved the thumb and pinkie." The digits wiggled at me. "And I understood that I would never run a corn harvester again. Not that I couldn't. I wouldn't."

"Scared?"

Malcolm snorted. "Nope. More like, well, that's done. Don't need to do it again. I started writing during rehabilitation. My first published piece was about a boy who buried three of his fingers. My next was about a boy who got a tattoo to cover a snakey scar that made its way from his wrist to his armpit. Then I started writing what I write now. Gothic stories inspired by the daily news." He leaned back. "Like today. Did you read about the--."

"Where is Rose?"

"How about a chess game?"

"Okay." I was being manipulated, but it wouldn't take long. Actually, I did better than I thought I would. He won, of course, but I received a hum of appreciation after several of my moves. When he checkmated me, I said, "Well?"

"She's in a little town outside of Pittsburgh. Her mother has cancer, and Rose has gone to be with her for a while." He paused, looked at me. "I have her telephone number. She wanted someone to know where she was."

Why hadn't she called me? Then I remembered that our conversation that ended in her telling me to fuck off. I couldn't imagine that Rose had ever told Malcom to fuck off.

"I think she meant you." Malcolm pointed a pinkie at me. "She knew you'd show up here asking for her. She was still ticked, you know, but she said she wanted you to know how ironic it all was. "

She meant her novel, of course, with the sick mother and the end-of-life reconciliation with her daughter and her boyfriend. Did that mean I was supposed to head East and join her and her mother as they stretched arms and hearts towards each other? One, was I her boyfriend? And two, wasn't her mother sick, probably not able to smoke pot or do anything else Rose had imagined in her story?

That was the trouble with fiction. Sometimes it's a lot more fun than real life. Besides, I still had a certain vignette in my memory, that same pinkie and thumb making its way through Rose's hair and trailing across her cheek. "Malcom, what's your role in all this?"

Malcolm's eyes were smiling again. "How about matchmaker?" He lifted his latte at me, took a sip, and raised his eyebrows.

I could never have been so Cary Grant. "You had your arm around her, your hand in her hair. You kissed her. That's matchmaking?"

"Entirely different matter. I was consoling a fellow artist. The day she gets her fifth rejection from an agent, she hears that her mother has become the protagonist in a drama Rose has only imagined. The book has become truth. And it isn't selling, no matter how true it is. My own books deal only with untruth, the victory of good over evil in a world populated by freaks. Much easier, the good over evil part, at least." He pushed a slip of paper towards me.

I took it and stood up. Malcolm settled in under the awning and said, "She really likes you, you know."

"Thanks, Malcolm. I'll be in for another game one of these nights."

When I finally got ahold of Rose, it was l:00 a.m. Eastern time and she sounded as if she had her blankets over her head. I apologized and asked if I should call in the morning. By that time, she had pulled herself upright and her words came through muffled but in English. "No," she said. "Give me a second." I could hear her swallowing water or something, cough, then, "Oh, Sam. I'm so glad you called. The scene here is deju vu all over again."

I grinned. She was still Rose, spunky. "Cliche, Rose. Yogi Berra. But it fits. How are you?"

We spent the next five minutes talking about the chemical smells of hospitals, of the stillness of sick mothers, of the strange ennui that sets in as one shares a room with an entubed body, watching for a twitch of an eye, a flicker of a toe. "I keep thinking of what I should have done, Sam. You know, the phone calls I didn't make, the invitations I never offered, the time I faked an excuse and missed Christmas because I couldn't stand to go through one more

"Silent Night" listening to my grandmother cry." Rose was crying now, so I waited. Rose was teaching me to wait.

"Sam?" She was back. "You were right about being destroyed but not defeated. My story is truthful. A daughter, at some point, after years of trying to disconnect, will try just as hard to connect with her mother. I'm just doing it a little late, that's all. I'm staying here until Mom is stabilized. I don't know how long that will be." She hesitated. "But I don't want to lose you, Sam. Do you understand?"

I let her words flow over me. I... don't...want...to...lose...you. They felt like warm fingers pressing into my temples; I held them there as long as I could. "I don't want to lose you, Rose," I whispered.

We didn't say anything more for a minute or two. Then Rose sighed. I could hear the pillow press against the phone, her voice distant, asleep. "Good night, Sam," she said.

"Good night, Rose," I answered even though I knew she hadn't heard me. As I hung up, I thought how like me it was to fall in love with someone who was three thousand miles away and perhaps not coming back for a long time.

The next morning, Mary didn't spare any words. "We have a problem, Sam, and it's you."

We had taken to meeting every Tuesday in the conference room at World Cup Cafe, at a table that could seat eight people, if necessary, coffee service a handwave away. This morning it was just Mary and Jane and me, at least this part of the session. I knew enough to look straight at Mary, ignoring the flitter of Jane's napkin against its scone, and said, " Okay, tell me."

"You've been impressive in your meetings with the politicos. They think you are an ice rink god and they'll follow you to the inner sanctum of the city council, if necessary. However, the money folks aren't so sure. I had hoped they wouldn't notice, but your credentials in terms of management leave something to be desired. They are wondering if perhaps we need to hire a bigger organization, one that has experience managing arenas, has some sort of success record, to put this piece of the project together."

I wanted to "Yes but" my way to absolution, like I used to when my mother got on my back about something. But Mary wasn't my mother and I wasn't sixteen. And I knew in my heart my critics were right. I had known it all along, that I wasn't the guy for this job, that I had a history of successful failures. Not just my marriage, although that two-year wander through stupidness was a part of the list. Right from the beginning, when I couldn't choose a toy for the $I.00 I had saved up without second thoughts and tears, in high school, when I couldn't stand not being perfect, so I didn't do anything, in college when I didn't make captain and walked away from a great team and into a drugged -out semi-pro organization. There, of course, I failed most successfully of all.

It was time to cave, admit the ride had been exciting, but was over.

"That's a good idea," I said. The words flowed from behind a hokey manly armor. I felt nothing but a tight band around my ribs. "I know a couple of national companies who run ice rinks. Maybe I could give someone their names?"

"These are the people to talk to." Mary handed me a list of my critics and stood up as the water bureau representative walked in, followed by the city councilor in charge of the utilities commission. I was dismissed.

The thing was, I wasn't having second thoughts. I was having first thoughts. I had spent the night awake and knowing that I needed to go to Pennsylvania to be with Rose. Not only needed, *wanted* to be in Bluefield with her. Rose was trying to be a daughter to a sick mother. I could relate, because I hadn't arrived at my own mother's bed until it was too late. And my dead mother was <u>still</u> trying to talk to me, to tell me whatever I hadn't been there to hear. "Sam" the stickie said. That's all. But her stories were like cave drawings, faint outlines to be wondered at. `Rose wanted more than post mortem guesses, and maybe I could help.

But it was more than that. Rose needed to stop guessing about me, too.

But not long distance, I knew that much. So, maybe it was meant to be that some of our backers didn't trust me and were looking around. Maybe it actually would work be okay. I'd give them the names of arena management companies I'd come in contact with during my hockey years and then I could leave, be with Rose, be free to start a new life, to make something different of myself. Everybody wins, right?

Except that the Living Room was a part of me. I knew exactly where the sales shop would be and what it would sell, and how the library would function, and why we needed a community meeting room. I even knew the color of the club chairs we'd have in the reading room, maroon, and how the cherry tables would expand for big community celebrations. I could see myself behind the food bar, mixing salads for the mothers, baking pizzas for the kids. Me, who flunked deep fryer 101. The entry's rubber floor would be black, the walls celadon green with maybe a touch of apricot on the woodwork. The girls' john stalls would be stainless steel; the boys' a tough black laminate. The acrylic windows looking onto the ice would be clear as glass. On the second floor, ticketholders to the shows and pro games would drink beer and eat Zenner bangers as they watched the action, clear-skinned servers moving among them with trays.

It was a good dream. I would be hard to give it up to a bunch of eastern professionals who didn't give shit about Zenner sausages. Or celedon green. Mrs. Jensen, my career counselor, had said that I was a risk taker, but the one thing I realized I couldn't risk was Rose. I knew that the moment I heard her voice last night. I choose her, I told myself, as I picked up the phone.

Rose had said decisions were like branches leading away from the trunk. Not ends, necessarily, just new directions. New leaves. We'd test that theory, in the next few days with the decisions I was making as I dialed Mary's list of board members and gave them the information they needed to look for a facility manager. I advised them to check references, ask if the company had ever been involved in a Living Room kind of development. Could they work with librarians as well as Zamboni drivers? And I wished them good luck.

I booked my flight to Pittsburgh for the next day. Rose met me at the airport and drove me to the little town of Bluefield and her mother's apartment. On the way she kept glancing at me as she pointed places we were passing: her old school, the corner she had her first car accident, a boyfriend's house. Finally, she stopped talking and pulled over.

"What's up, Sam?"

"I love you," I answered, like it was something I said every day. As I kissed her, I realized I had been saying it everyday for a long time, practicing .

"Oh, Sam," she answered, her voice vibrating in my ear. "Isn't this fun?"

"Way fun," I answered. "But we have to talk first."

"Oh, god," she whispered.

"No, not like that. I don't think. It will be up to you."

And then I told her about me, about the stones in my craw, about a deadly five seconds that poisoned a marriage, derailed a life. And when I was through mixing up metaphors, avoiding the real words, I told her the truth.

"I killed someone. A kid, really, younger than me, who was trying to prove himself, maybe be perfect, so he could follow his dream, go to the big time. A lot like me, only still a kid. Afterwards, his mother told me about him and I held her hand and told her how sorry I was, and she said she forgave me, but I didn't believe her. How could she ever forgive me? Her cool skin against mine reminded me of my mother, crying, being brave, like mothers are supposed to be."

"Sam--"

"He'd come at me, his stickup high, too high, caught me across the nose. I was bleeding and mad as hell. His team was in the cellar and we were headed toward the playoffs, and our heads weren't in the game. Even though we had outshot them 42-12, we were one goal behind with a minute and a half to go, which made me mad, too. We should have been ahead by five, and I was blaming everyone. We had the puck and the other team had fallen into a trap defense wall just beyond the blue line. Todd looked at me and forwarded the puck out to the left winger. I raced down the right side. The left winger dumped it deep behind the net where I circled, waiting for it. Pete , our center, cycled behind me . Then I saw that this kid, the one who'd caught me with his stick, was going for the puck from the other side and was heading right at me. Pete could have the puck. I would get the kid. I dropped my shoulder and aimed my body at him and hit him so hard against the boards I lost my balance. He slid down the boards and fell to the ice, me on top of him. I got up. He didn't.

"The refs stopped the game, gathered around him, and I heard myself yelling, "It was a clean hit. You saw that!" By now, the refs were kneeling, unfastening his helmet. One of the looked up at me and told me to shut up. Pete and Todd grabbed me, hauled me away, back to our bench. I didn't want to sit. I wanted to go to the kid, tell him to get up, stop faking it, pansy, but someone pushed me down and I realized the crowd was no longer quiet, like it gets when someone is hurt. Boos and calls and my name like a dirty word hailed down on us as the medics lifted the kid's body onto the stretcher. "Clean hit," I kept saying to the backs of my teammates leaning on the rail, watching. "Clean hit". Then the applause began, silenced the shouting, as if clapping hands might wake the kid up as he was carried out.

"He was dead. I knew that the second I saw his open eyes, his neck twisted, his head resting against a shoulder pad. And I had done it."

"Sam, god Sam, I can't imagine how you felt."

"For a while, every time I let my mind loose I saw the kid coming at me, I felt my shoulder meet his chest, watched him crumble, a tape loop that never stopped except when I was drunk or asleep or forcing myself to read. I took a leave from the team, holed up, avoided my teammates who finally stopped calling. I got sick every t me I thought about getting on the ice."

"Then you played again? Later?"

"The next season, I dropped down a league, coached a little.

Every kid I looked at looked like him. I couldn't do it. I quit. Then I met Reba."

Reba looks me and shakes her head. "Your wallowing, Babe," she says in her Georgia accent. "You need a good shaking, get you back on track." She grins like she's the one who is going to do it. We are in her bed, I am drunk, unable to do anything but cry and babble.

"I've already been shook up. That's the trouble," I say. "It was a clean hit."

Reba just lays her head on my chest and pats my shoulder. "It's okay," she says and I want to begin to believe her.

Three weeks later she has me drinking less, running, laughing at her cornball jokes sometimes. It is winter, Iowa, and there is a pond in the park. I teach her how to skate. We skate until spring. Now the tape only runs at the first moment of sleep, of waking, shuts down most of the day. Even the sound of the ice doesn't activate it except in odd, clumsy moments as a stranger glides toward me.

I ask her to live with me. "On what?" she asks. She's right. I get a job as a children's league coach, also desk duty, program manager at a local rink, enough to plan on. I ask again and she says yes. We start dreaming, decide to get married in Parkdale, and my mom and sister and my buddies like her. "She's a keeper," they say.

In our new house, when I wake up at night with a yell, she puts her head on my chest and chants "Clean hit, baby" until I go back to sleep. She doesn't understand much about hockey, but she thinks she understands me. She wants me to play pro again. "To be yourself again," she says. And maybe part of me wants to be myself again, too, but that kid's crooked neck stops me from dialing, getting in touch with people.

Reba keeps urging, "You just have to get off your duff, Babe. You still got it." I get mad at her, accuse her of not loving me, just wanting to be a hockey wife.

By now I'm working in construction, the tape pretty quiet. Not much money, though, if that's what she wants. I start drinking more, missing dinner, all that shit. I get laid off and Reba goes to work. "This is not what I call married," she says. "It's more like childcare."

Two years later Reba leaves. For good reason. I go live with my mother until neither of us can stand me anymore. I take a job as handyman at Silver Skates, move into the garage house, drink beer and read books, get fired, live on unemployment. I realize the tape is still going, but subliminally now, like the ringing in your ears that you don't hear except when you listen hard.

I didn't say all this to Rose, of course. Except how the kid was permanently embedded in my life, making a normal life impossible.

"Reba left because I was sure I couldn't be a husband or anything else and I set out to prove it, no matter what she did to convince me otherwise.

"And you left the Comstock plan because....?

"Probably for the same reason. I'm flawed goods, Rose. You need to know that." I pulled away from her, thought about the truth of it, how I'd always been flawed goods, even a long time ago, even in the backseat of the car, holding my toy, wondering if I could have done chosen better. Even when my mother told me of my father's leaving and I made a joke, even as I hit that kid too hard and yelled "Clean hit."

Rose was silent, huddled in the corner of the seat, her eyes closed. I imagined that in a moment she would reach for the keys, start the car, pull a U, take me back to the airport. Better now than later, I told myself. Before we start dreaming. I felt her hand take mine, her warm fingers pressing my cold palm.

"Dear Sam. We're all flawed goods. Haven't you figured that out by now?" She shook her head, like she couldn't believe me. "My god, that's why I write, to examine the flaws. That's why people do good things, to mend them. That's why people become CEO's, President, Oprah, to cut around them, make something out of the fabric despite the flaws. If we ignore or deny them, we become blind to ourselves, to others. They are what allow us to forgive, hope, love." Rose took a big breath, waited for her words to sink in and for me to respond.

It would take a while. Maybe a long while. In the meantime, I let her know I had heard what she said, that I loved her for it. I kissed her, held her tight.

Then she pulled away from me and started the car.

"Later," she said. She was smiling.

The apartment smelled of roses and maybe a cat. The living room was cheek-to-jowl in lamps and blond furniture. Heywood Wakefield, Rose said, like I should know. An overstuffed sofa and matching green tweed swivel chairs flanked a mahogany console and its gray screen. I would sleep on the sofa, Rose said. She was using her mother's bedroom until she came back from the hospital. No, we couldn't, she frowned, when I looked at her. Mom's bed was off limits. So we made love on the sofa, eager, no words, until I fell to the floor and jammed my elbow on the Heywood-Wakefield coffee table. Then we laughed and she came down, too, and we continued between softly curved blond legs. "Careful," Rose said, finally, and we wriggled our ways to safety.

Then we went to the hospital. Rose's mother reminded me of a bowl of bread pudding, soft, sweet, revealing an occasional raisin of humor, despite the tubes. She wanted to know who I was, and I wanted to know the same about her. So we asked questions and told stories. "I remember my first boyfriend," she said. "He asked my father for permission to take me to the Lutheran talent show. He played his ukulele and I thought he was grand until he started to sing. It was good I heard him sing right off or I might have wasted months on him." She looked bright-eyed at me. "Do you sing?"

Rose said, "No, but he writes." She winked at me.

The next few days slipped by, Rose at the hospital most of the time, I cooking dinner, listening, visiting in her awake-hours with Annie. When she was up to it, we'd try a game of gin, her tubes knocking over piles of cards, her hee-hees making me laugh in the midst of defeat. She was a good older woman. Not like my mother, not a questioning person, but someone you'd like to find in your kitchen lifting a pot roast out of the oven. "I remember when Rose was born. I wondered if I had eaten something I shouldn't have while she was growing in me, she was so awake, her eyes looking around, her arms reaching and reaching. She's not changed, has she?" Annie turned her gaze towards Rose's coal black hair. "She says it will look good on the cover of her novel. What do you think?"

"I don't think she's changed."

"And are you two going to get married?"

Rose and I looked at each other, then at Annie. We knew what she wanted us to say. I let Rose say it. "We might, Mom. We're thinking about it."

"Don't think too hard, Rosie. Somethings don't require thinking. You know that, Rose." Then Annie slipped back on her pillow and shut her eyes.

Rose and I left the room and headed for the coffee shop in the basement of the hospital. I hated hospital cafeterias. No one except the few green-uniformed anestheologists and surgeons was there for any good reason. "What did your mother mean? About not thinking?" I asked, when we found a table in the sad-faced room.

Rose sat back, put her hands around the warm paper cup in front of her. "I think she was remembering something, a time right after my father died when I was maybe eighteen, mom was fifty or so, the other kids barely home and not caring about being there. Mom met a man, Harold. He wasn't like my father in any way. Dad was tall and handsome with a black mustache, quick to laugh and even quicker to yell. We kids walked around him, avoiding unnecessary contact unless he was smiling. After he got sick, he stayed in his room most of the time, avoiding us. Sometimes we could hear him groaning curses, ringing his bell for Mom. Even then, she took the brunt of his anger. When it came time for me to leave home, I did, only not the way my father wanted me to. He died during the year I lived with the guitar player."

"Not Malcolm," I said, hoping for a smile.

Rose was remembering too hard to be interrupted. "Harold and Mom met at church, maybe even before Dad died. Afterwards, Harold began calling on my mother and sometimes she'd mention going somewhere with this nice man. I came home for a while after the guitar player and I split up, and the nice man turned out to be about twenty years older than Mom, short, round, and always in a white shirt and tie. His scalp glowed. I wondered if he polished it.

"'Well, how do you like him?' Mom asked me at breakfast one morning. She was holding a birthday card Harold had sent, fanning herself a little with it.

"I knew enough, at least, not to comment on his looks. 'He's very. . .nice, like you said. He seems like he'd be handy to do things with, you know, go places with. I appreciated the way he asked how I was feeling, 'Emotionwise,' he said. Do you like him?'

"My mother hesitated, looked away. 'I think I do. He's kind. He says he cares for me. That's important, isn't it?'

"'Yes.'

"'I've thought about it a lot. There's something, I don't know. . .'

"I wanted to say it for her. Sex. My dad had been sexy. I knew, the way kids know. Harold wasn't, but 'at fifty five, does it matter so much any more?' I finally asked.

"'You don't know much, do you?' she answered.

"A couple of months later Mom wrote that she had 'broken up' with Harold. He, not too devastated, was already seeing another widow from church. 'I think he just wants a nurse for his old age,' Mom wrote. 'I've done that. Never again.' I could imagine her lifting a determined chin. A year after he married the other widow, he died and left her a half million dollars. It was years before Mom could laugh about it."

"Does she think I'll be leaving you a fortune? That's why you shouldn't think too much?"

Rose drained her cup, grinned. "I think she was referring to the sex part."

In our quiet moments at night, Rose would put her head on my chest and pat my shoulder. "It's going to be all right," she would whisper and I wondered how women knew to do that.

Annie decided not to die. When we came to visit, we'd find her clunking down the linoleum lined hall, her walker making little hops, her feet shushing in their soft slippers. She was sent to a rehab facility, which she hated. "They come in at all hours and make me breathe into this plastic thing or pee or take a pill. The food is terrible. I want to come home." So we gathered all of her plastic items including the breathing thing, ("Leave it here," she commanded, but the aide wouldn't let us) and brought her back to her apartment.

The sofa reverted to Rose, who would stay on until she could arrange a visiting nurse and a housekeeper for her mother. And a cat. The old calico had disappeared the day I moved in. Rose also wanted time to ask about Harold, about her father, about sex, she admitted. She was imagining a novel, one in which the mother lives. Conversations like those would go better in the privacy of her mother's bedroom, over the whiskey-laced hot toddy which had taken the place of a couple of the pills. I would go back to the west coast to work out what I would do next, jobwise. The new kitten, gray, fearless, a lamp climber, reminded me the day I left that there was also a tree metaphor about being out on a limb.

CHAPTER SEVENTEEN

Three week's of mail made my first step into my apartment a dangerous one. A crazed phone blinked in the dark. My refrigerator smelled godawful along with most of my clothes. I was hungry. I shut the door and headed for Shaker's, a beer and a burger, and an unreal moment before I re-entered my real life.

"Shit! Where you been, man?"

I grabbed Davie's fist and pumped it. Over his shoulder I saw Todd and Jake.

They raised their bottles at me and grinned. "Hey," they said. They had regrouped after Barney's wedding.

What could I tell them? What did I want to tell them? Besides, it was Stanley Cup time. I waved for a beer and sat back to watch the NHL semi-finals. Talk about deja vu all over again. Except for the hockey game itself, though, it wasn't. I glanced at the three of them. Barney was AWOL, as usual, paying attention to the other part of his life. Jake was wearing a sports jacket, a tie, his cell phone in easy reach on his belt. Davie, getting fat, shouldn't lean forward like that on a bar stool, showing his butt crack. Todd's gray skin and slow eyelids straight out of *Night of the Living Dead*. I don't know how they saw me, but I suspected they believed they were looking at a dirty-T-shirt has-been. All the four of us had in common were a thousand or so games. Tonight, however, that was enough. "Bring me a Big Daddy," I ordered. "I'm starved."

I walked home after the game. The air was rain-washed and clean. The rhodies, as old as the ancient houses they leaned against, glowed pink and purple under the white, clouded night sky. For a minute or so, my neighborhood lived up to the dream we had had for it. Then the booming rap beat thudding from the car slithering by me, windows down, guys looking me over, brought my life into focus, and I picked up my pace and was glad when I reached my front door.

I wasn't ready to listen to the phone messages or to tear open the envelopes from Mercy Corps and Right to Die and Quest, whatever. I went to bed, noting a need to visit the laundromat. Tomorrow.

At 11:30 pm the phone rang. It was 2:30 a.m. EST. Rose? I answered. My sister wailed, "Thank god. I've been calling for days. Where have you been?"

"Did you ever imagine I might be dead?" I answered. "I didn't notice any evidence of your forced entry." I shoved myself to sitting position. "So I'm home. What?"

"You don't know, do you? About the arena? About the project? It was in all the papers. They're say it's a boondoggle. Favored contractors and inside investors out to make millions. A sure failure in a bad part of town. They are going for a stop order on all plans." Sharon paused to breathe.

"Who's they?"

"The other side, of course. Politicians who weren't in on the plans; realtors who feel left out. Even the mayor, who had ideas about another neighborhood, plans for a sports center she wants built in S.E., an Olympic pool. When Mary Perry got a matching grant for the park, all hell broke loose."

"Guess I'm glad I missed it." I closed my eyes and tried to bring back the beery calm I'd been dogpaddling in.

"Sam!"

"I'm not involved in the arena any more, Sharon. I left for Pennsylvania and Rose three weeks ago after giving the arena back to the Board of Directors."

"You didn't call me."

"No. I almost did." That day, the day I made the calls to the Board, handed the Living Room over to them, flew away, I spent the three-hour flight to Chicago wrestling with doubts. During the layover in O'Hare I took out my cell phone, thinking Sharon might be able to nudge me in one direction or another, off the railing I perched on, arms flailing: black-haired girl on one side, a good fight on the other. Deserting the fight felt as bad as having to sit out the last three minutes of a game. Sharon would say I was running away again. I should go back, take the gloves off, throw a few punches. Then I thought of Rose, the way she made me feel whole, the way she filled my empty places with her laughter, the way my stomach flipped just thinking of her in that noisy airport, cell phone in one hand, boarding pass in the other.

Then I thought about me, what I hadn't admitted to myself or to anyone else for a long time. I was a man riddled with terminal self-doubt. Always had been. Mom called them second thoughts. When I was six my mother had explained them to me as I curled up in the back seat of the car next to the groceries and cried, sure I'd made a mistake buying a Hot Wheels car instead of a wrist rocket with my allowance. She told me I was prone to second thoughts because I was especially aware of all the possibilities in the world and had trouble settling on just one. It was a gift, in a way, she said, and a hindrance in another. Knowing possibilities allowed a person to dream big. Second thoughts meant you were acting on that dream and a little worried about the narrowing road. Just breathe, she said, and take the next step. When I was little, the next step was to take the car out of its box, feel its smooth edges, tuck it in my pocket and make it mine.

As I got older, the next steps were to skate fast, hit hard, yell the doubts into submission, drown them with beer. Until the kid.

At that in the airport lounge, remembering, I breathed, put away the phone, got into line when my flight was called, sat back and waited for whatever was to be to happen.

"No, I didn't, Sharon. I had to work out things for myself, and I did, we did, Rose and me, I mean. "

"And?"

"We're good." I didn't want to say any more right then, too out of it to make sense of anything. Maybe the whole Comstock dream **had** been just a scheme to make money. Maybe Mary and Jane were the front women for a gang of greedy investors out to feed from the public trough. I was probably lucky to get out when I did. "I'll call you," I said into the silence at the other end of the line.

Sharon hung up. No point in trying to sleep. I opened the last beer in the fridge and began listening to my messages. Sharon, of course, until clicks indicated she hadn't waited for the recording to answer. A couple of solicitors, a wrong message, and a patient voice, calling daily : "When you get in, Sam, give me a call." Mary's last message came at 9:30 a.m. that day. The part of me that didn't believe the conspiracy theory dialed her number. As her answering service came on, Mary's unrecorded voice broke through. "Sam," she said. "I'm so glad you called," as if was two in the afternoon, not in the morning. "You've been away."

"I just got in," I lied. "I heard a little about what's been going on. How are you doing?" I really wanted to know.

"Fine. It's a mess, though, and we need you." Katharine Hepburn, clear and crisp as if she never slept. "Breakfast at my house, tomorrow at 8:00 a.m."

She had no doubt I'd be there, and neither did I.

Mary's home in the West Hills overlooked the city, a clapboard two-story white colonial with a widow's walk resting on the crest of its shingled roof. She met me at the door and led me through the dining room, across a deep red carpet and under a crystal chandelier, and into the large kitchen. The table, in a sunlit nook, was set for two, cloth napkins and a small bouquet of red tulips waiting for us. "From my garden," she said. "Keeps me sane these days." She took a pan from the oven. "Hope you like vegetables. Frittata." She cut into the egg pie and offered me a plate. "Rolls and fruit on the table." Then she sat down across from me and said, "We are going to win this one, Sam."

Cutting and chewing in her careful way, she described how we would do it. Her operatives were, as we spoke, gathering evidence that the mayor and her buddies were about to use pressure to change the zoning on a large piece of land in Southeast Parkland, now protected by land use laws, so that a consortium of three builders, two banks, and the city's largest realtor could build a "model" suburb. This development would be designed to look as if it had always been part of the city, with cozy shops, restaurants, multiple-occupancy dwellings, and single family houses. The new neighborhood would have a community center and swimming pool. It sounded great in theory.

However, there were problems. Besides the zoning change which would impact agriculture beyond the land use boundary, the new development would require roads, sewers, water, and all the rest of the infrastructure that would make it livable. The city would have to pay for these improvements, as well as offer low-interest loans for some of the housing. The cost to the city could be in the triple-digit millions. Not accountable in terms of money were the loss of wetlands, a section of forest, and the farming lands that not only supported families but were homes to a world of wild life.

"All they need to get is a zoning change," Mary said. "The mayor is gathering support by claiming the city is overcrowded, and housing stock is so limited and expensive that people are moving to the suburbs. She hints at the possibility of light rail being built in that direction if the Feds go for it, and she's enlisted one of our Representatives to lobby for funds."

Mary carried our empty plates to the sink and turned back to look at me. "You understand that our plan to renovate Comstock would do exactly the same thing: offer housing and jobs and a place for families and businesses and easy access to the center of town, at a fraction of the cost to the city. And at the same time, a dead neighborhood will be revived without impacting the environment, the farmers, or the integrity of the folks who are supposed to be holding the line on land use in this town. We can do it all, but the attack on our plan is vicious. Several of our board members have backed out because they don't want to be painted with the same brush that's coloring us." She paused. "Coffee?" she asked, pointing at the coffeemaker.

I nodded, glad for a moment to take a breath, consider the situation. I'm just a guy who likes ice, I told myself. Second thoughts,

I told myself. For good reason, I realized. "Mary, before we go any further, you need to know something about me."

"I think I already know, Sam. The accident." She smiled in a calm sort of way. "So does Jane. We Googled you. Months ago. Took a little patience. You were way down the line, timewise and importance wise."

Breathe. Observe the narrowing road. As she put the cup in front of me, I was ready to ask, "What can I do?"

Mary was prepared for the question. "We need community organization. We need people who live in the Comstock neighborhood to rise up and support the idea of renovation, of ownership, of clean streets and a safe playground. We need someone to rile them up."

She smiled. "Think of it as a hockey game, last period, tied 2 -2, you've got the puck. Involves passing and a plan, and a team who can skate fast. I think you can do it, Sam. Will you try? By the way," she added, "those big management companies you suggested? None of them, to the surprise of the board, got the Living Room idea, especially the library. You knew they wouldn't, didn't you?" Before I could answer she added, "So did I."

A day or so later, I shined up my leather shoes for the house visits and meetings with business guys in short sleeves and khakis. And in between, the schedule on my PalmPilot, I stopped at Coffee Tyme in my sweats. This time I bribed Malcolm. I'd play to win if he'd hear me out first. He did, and he agreed to be on my committee: Resuscitate Our Neighborhood, RON. After beating me again, he brought in a couple of coffee house regulars, artists who designed posters, and he agreed to write the press release for the neighborhood meeting to be held on the site of the would-be playground.

I went back to Shaker's on a game night and got Todd and Jake off their stools and stapling posters on telephone poles. Then people I had never met began calling and asking how they could help; neighbors who had nearly given up hope. Several called to complain about drug houses. I told them I couldn't do anything about them right then, but it wouldn't be long before the neighborhood itself drove them out. Come to the meeting, I said.

And they did, three hundred of us, on a warm spring evening, lounging on old blankets and lawn chairs. A speaker system from the mall's Radio Shack overcame the low moan of the freeway a couple of blocks away, and two black-and-white-cow persons from Ben and Jerry's handed out ice cream and mooed. People laughed and little kids kicked lumps of newly-cut grass, courtesy of my neighbor with the lawn mower, at each other. Then I stood in front of the microphone, counting, l-2-3, and cleared my throat. I noticed a photographer and a woman in a red dress talking to folks in the crowd. The media, I guessed.

Then it was time, and people quieted and looked up at me. The speech I had practiced in bed the night before melted away like a dream the moment I raised my arms. So I free skated. I said what a wonderful warm evening, what friendly faces, how neighborly the scene was. I got my wind and said how proud I was of being included in a project that would make life-defining changes to everyone sitting in the grass, to everyone living in Comstock. I was beginning to enjoy the sound of my voice, could have gone on, but Mary and Jane had come forward, were standing at my side. Another time, I thought, and I introduced them as the two woman who had changed my life. and would change everyone else's who was listening.

Mary spoke and Jane nodded. They told of their plans for their old neighborhood which they were determined to revitalize. They explained how they expected to finance the project, how they had chosen the contractors and advisors who formed their board, and how they wished to include the ideas and the dreams of the people who lived in the area. They described the Living Room, the heart of the project, the meeting place for families and children, and they pointed to me, saying I had dreamt the first dream and would be making sure it happened. I waved. I enjoyed the sound of hands clapping.

"We are asking the city only for improved roads and sidewalks and the repair of water and sewer lines, the same maintenance any older neighborhood would expect. We ask its help in approaching the federal government for mortgage assistance for those wishing to buy into the neighborhood. We have lined up several financial institutions who are willing to work with us on individual home improvement loans to owners. A grant will cover the cost of planning and the construction of a new park, the ground on which you are sitting. We are talking with the school district about a small elementary school in the old building that has stood empty for years. If that doesn't work out, we have had inquiries from several charter schools who are interested in using the building if RON takes off. The possibilities are limitless. But we need your help," Mary said, her voice strong and clear. "If you want this project to take place, you need to attend the City Council meeting next week." She and Jane walked from the microphone in a swirl of applause and excited voices.

Then Coffee Tyme regulars began handing out informational letters with city council members' addresses, e-mail and telephone numbers and those of the new headquarters of RON. I glanced at it and looked at Mary.

"We bought it," she whispered, as the applause died down and people started talking to each other and rolling up blankets. Mary and Jane, their organization, owned the ice rink. RON would be located in Lou's old office. Among my duties, she added, would be the management the rink, at least until the project settled down and we could begin renovation in earnest.

All we needed now was to defeat the mayor.

"Can I help? Pro bono?" My father's voice. "You've got an exciting tiger by the tail." He had caught up us as we walked towards the rink, asking all three of us, looking at me, grinning.

All I needed was for Rose to come home. We talked every night: her mother was going to the toilet by herself; she was using a cane and walking a block; she had cooked them dinner; she washed her own hair. Rose was finding time to write and send out her novel, in its fourth revision, to agents, but since they wouldn't answer for months, she had no feedback. "It's like tossing a stone in a well and waiting for the splash, except that it doesn't. I'm giving them my apartment address and the Post Office is holding my mail, so I figure that by the time I get back, I'll have about thirteen rejections. Are you ready for that?"

I was ready for Rose, no matter. I hadn't seen her for more than three weeks;

I could go back to Pennsylvania, but I was wheeling along this narrow road that now included the rink and I needed to be there every day to steer.

The first thing I did was raise the wages of the Zamboni driver, Max. I also found out that he could line the ice, maintain the refrigeration equipment and manage the light and sound system. So I put him on a yearly salary with benefits to insure his loyalty.

I talked with the pimply kid at the bar and advised him to keep his fingers off his face. I hired a front desk girl with a smile and a frisky attitude. She also knew computers and during her slow hours, she databased our mailing list and Quickened our accounts.

I hired out the housekeeping to a team of local women who were eager to clean up the girls' lavatory and their mouths, if possible. Todd brought in his crew of nursery workers and the bark dust, and rhododendrons replaced the jungle of weeds. I bit the budget bullet, and clear acrylic windows looked onto the ice. Malcolm designed a brochure and distributed it to the nearby PTA's, offering special group rates for classes and ice time. We offered child care on Thursday mornings for mothers who wanted a morning out, and a couple of Coffee Tyme regulars were happy to earn money babysitting when the mothers began showing up, two by two.

I myself painted the front doors an inviting celadon. The arena wasn't perfect, but recreational skaters were trickling in.

The other lane of my narrow road was not as smooth. The council meeting to discuss plans for both urban developments was scheduled for April 2, then postponed until April 12. This, I guessed, was to throw the Comstock community off. We'd received good newspaper coverage for our first meeting and thirty seconds on the local news channel. Reporters had been alerted to the council meeting, and from what we could tell, people were ready to come downtown to attend. We weren't sure what the ten-days' delay would mean. We alluded to conspiracy in the door-to-door hand-out we distributed, we were not beyond that kind of tactic, and urged families to bring babies and grandparents.

The agenda had Comstock down for 2:00. By 2:30 the babies were getting restless. We guessed that at least a hundred people had shown up, and Mary was pleased but nervous, fidgeting with couple of folders on her lap. As we waited for the council members to appear, she told me that she had firm evidence of the collusion between certain contractors and developers and the mayor's office, a cloakroom set of agreements intended to force the district land-use office into negotiations to change the boundaries for development. The agreements involved an exchange of non-buildable hilly property in NW for the SE section they wanted to rezone, the wetlands as flat as a developer would ever hope for. Mary didn't want to use the folder unless she had to. This was not the time to make enemies, she said.

At 2:35, the council members straggled into the chambers, glanced at the motley group looking back at them and found their chairs. The mayor, who seemed more pink that usual, her forehead shiny despite the layer of cloudy makeup, coughed into the microphone. The air in the room thinned as a hundred or so people inhaled. "It has become apparent," the mayor said in an unexpected tiny voice, "that the strong interest in the welfare of the environment, a trait of every Oregonian, as we all know, must be respected. The council will not proceed with the development of the SE parcel."

A communal exhale accompanied by startled laughter and applause restored the air quality in the room.

Mary smiled and rearranged her folders. The one on top now was labeled RON, The Best Thing About to Happen in Our City. We were next on the agenda. Mary rose, walked to the microphone set up in the aisle for common folk. She spoke fervently, introduced Jane, whose words wandered a little in support of her friend, her business suit was more impressive than her speech, and then it was my turn.

I'd had a taste of being amplified. And also a taste of what it felt like to have one's words lift off, take wing, move solemn-eyed listeners to action. I liked it. I liked what words could do, the energy they could loosen, the branches and limbs of change that sprouted in their path.

"This weekend," I said, "I borrowed a lawn mower from my neighbor and mowed my lawn. I planted two rhodies and a row of busy lizzies on the shady side of the house. When I finished, I sanded my front door and painted it the best color I know, celadon green. Then I pulled back my curtains and washed my windows, a task new to me, but I remembered my mother's wadded up pads of newsprint, and I polished each pane like she used to. My little house, a garage house, I used to call it, is beginning to be a pretty good-looking home.

"Why did I do it? Because, for the first time in years, I am proud of where I live. I'm proud of my street's possibilities, and I'm proud of my neighbors, who have come today to meet you. They, and I, have found hope in RON, and it has changed the way we look at our community. We are ready to get to work.

"We ask for our city's support. We're not asking for millions of dollars. We ask for the usual help that any neighborhood deserves as roads and sewers and pipes age. We ask for the expertise of your specialists as we move through regulations and funding. We are asking for the council's backing as we approach the state and federal government for help. We ask, most of all, that you believe in our plan and in the committed people who are working for its success."

I turned to the audience. "Will everyone involved in RON's committees and work forces please stand?" Guys in suits and gold watches rose along with a half dozen Coffee Tyme regulars and a couple managers of shops in the mall. Then the mother with the fussing baby stood up, and then the older man with the lawnmower who lived down the block from me. A woman in a wheel chair raised her arm. Then almost everyone in the room stood up, and they smiled and applauded themselves and sent pleased grins to their neighbors. I turned back to the five council members and the mayor and said, "See what I mean? We're all in on this. This is a win-win situation for each person in this room, including the five of you."

When the audience settled down again, the council asked for an official proposal from the RON organization, Mary handed her folder to the mayor. The plan had been written by her attorney, a former member of the city council, adept in the format. The council received it, referred it to the next meeting's agenda, and thanked everyone for coming. Our fifteen minutes in the spotlight were over.

I could hardly wait to get to the lobby. "How did you get them to give up on the SE project, Mary?"

She gave me her prim smile, said, "I didn't. Jane did" She pressed a finger over her lips, nodded toward the crowd around us. When we got to her car, she invited me in and explained. "Jane's former husband, Bill Nixon, is one of the mayor's largest contributors. He believes that the mayor's good for business, unlike her past opponents who have supported higher business taxes to fund health care and the homeless. However, his replacement wife is on the board of The Nature Conservancy and the National Audubon Society and that's where her own money and energy is directed. I can't imagine some of their pillow conversations. Can you? "Apparently a recent phone call from ex-wife Jane to now-wife Elizabeth inspired a change of heart on the part of Bill. During that call, Jane suggested that the Conservancy may want to purchase the SE section before the developers got ahold of it. The wetlands, fed by a spring, a tributary of Johnson Creek, were the winter rearing habitat of the endangered Coho salmon, which spend the first year of their lives in its waters. So close to an urban area, Jane said, so valuable for the city children to experience."

I couldn't imagine it. "The ex-wives talk to each other?"

"Of course. They are in the same pitch club."

I didn't ask.

Bill Nixon was no fool. Two wives of the same mind meant hell on earth if he didn't go along with them. Nixon's money and his ability to raise a lot more in this election year overwhelmed the promises of the developers. As for the mayor, backing down would result in a calmer term of office than if she had to deal with a festering neighborhood sore spot. Perhaps she would even take credit for making RON a reality. Such were my thoughts as I headed back to my green yard and green front door. I missed Rose. I wanted to preen, fan my finny tail at her, scrape out a hole in the gravel. An ecological thing. Hard to do over the phone.

CHAPTER EIGHTEEN

The flashing red button wasn't Rose. Sharon needed to talk. Could we meet, maybe at my house while Will is in school? She'd arrange a play date for Enid. Today? I looked at my watch: it was already a quarter to five. We had missed the playdate. I called and told her to come over whenever. I would be home, folding my laundry.

"Okay," she said. "I'll get Han to stay later if I can."

When she knocked on the door I was holding a sock in my hand, wondering why I had holes in the heels of every pair I owned.

"You have a nail," Sharon answered as I poked a finger through the worn spot at her. "Check your shoes. The leather ones, not the Adidas."

That's why I liked having an older sister. She knew everything, except the answer to the question she asked as we leaned back, glasses of wine at hand, a sense of siblingness warming us.

"Why do I want him back? I've taken this righteous position, this 'I can do this myself!' stance, and I know that I can. I don't need him to get on with life. I have a part time job, the kids are okay, I feel very much myself. But, Sam, every time I hear a car go by the house, every time the phone rings, I hope it's Wilfred." Her eyes were shiny, but her voice didn't waver. "Sometimes I dream that he's breathing beside me and I reach out and his pillow's cold." She sipped her wine, closed her eyes for a moment.

I could have answered that I used to feel that way about Reba, too, but the feeling finally subsided into a sliver of regret, then a small scar. I could tell her that Wilfred's ghost would slither away after a while, hide in some secret cave, his place in her life filled by others offering promises and laughter.

Then I thought of Enid and Will. Even though I was mostly grown when our parents divorced, if anyone had asked what I wanted out of life, and I felt like being honest, I would have answered, "I want to have my family back." I think I needed to know, as I groped for a hold on life, that at least one of my feet was on solid ground. I used to imagine Dad moving back in, telling me to chew with my mouth closed, Mom and him having their quiet arguments behind their bedroom door, Sharon and I setting each other off just to see what our parents would do and to whom. Like the time we were wrestling in the kitchen, yelling at each other, and my mother swung around and hit me across the nose with the trout she had been flouring, and my dad grabbed her arm and accused her of fish abuse. That's what I wanted back and never got.

Sharon's kids deserved a second chance at being the family they believed they once were.

"You still love him, Sharon." I said. "Ask him to come back."

"You can't be serious. I haven't talked to him in a month. He just picks up the kids and takes them to McDonalds."

"McDonalds is good. Means he's loosened up a little." I moved over to her side of the sofa. "Talk to him," I said. I almost added, "If you don't, you'll always regret it." But I didn't. Who knows what regrets a person will hunker over? And what regrets will finally melt away in the night, a black-haired rosemary-scented head on one's shoulder. Damn, I missed her. "Give it a try. Say you will."

My sister went to the kitchen for another glass of wine, and came back with the bottle and something else on her mind. She looked at the iMac. "Feels like Mom is saying that, too." She filled my glass and said, "I know who Adrienne was." She held out her hand to me. The ruby ring encircled her middle finger.

"Dad told me. Adrienne taught with Mom years ago. The two couples went out once in a while, but it was the women who were friends. They stayed friends even when Mom stopped working to take care of us. She went back to teaching in a different school, and the friendship faltered. Then one day the phone rang and it was Adrienne, in tears. Her husband had just gotten on a plane for Austin, heading for a new life with a young man he had been seeing in a rented apartment for a year. He'd come out with a bang, announcing the reason for his quitting his job at a staff meeting of fellow engineers. He walked out and never looked back"

"Even then? I thought it had something to do with fluoride in the water."

Sharon ignored my attempt at humor. "There's more." The red stone shone like a drop of the wine she sipped. "Adrienne was completely destroyed by her husband's rejection. She took a leave from teaching, stayed in her bedroom for several months, her house fell into shambles. Mom took to visiting her after school, bringing her food, doing the laundry. Slowly Adrienne pulled herself together. She planted some flowers. She started caring about the house and herself. Mom's visits became times to share a glass of wine, to talk and laugh. Sometimes she'd come home a little drunk."

"I don't remember any Adrienne. We must have met her."

"Dad says we didn't. He didn't want to get involved in Adrienne's problems. He hadn't liked the husband much either. So the renewed friendship wasn't really on his radar screen. Then one day Mom walked in very upset, and when Dad insisted, she told him that Adrienne had said that she loved her and had kissed her. Dad laughed it off. He suggested that homosexuality must be catching in that family. Mom's answer was, 'Is there an inoculation for it?'"

"Shit."

"Mom started coming home right after school; she never mentioned Adrienne again. Neither did Dad. "

"The ring?"

"Adrienne died about the time Mom and Dad separated. Dad thinks Adrienne left the ring to Mom. He thought it was probably her engagement ring."

So the Always had been explained. Always, Adrienne? A promise to Adrienne, not from her. Mom's sexual encounter with Adrienne was understandable, at least in the retelling. So why was my sister looking at me in that superior way, like I wasn't getting it?

"You aren't getting it, are you? Mom was haunted by the almostness, the possibilities of that kiss. She wrote about it, in the beach story where she imagined a night of sex with Adrien. After she wrote about the breakup of her marriage, an imagined fling with a stranger, writing that eased the pain."

"No way, Sharon. Not Mom."

"She was ready for a new experience. In her head, like always. People live in a million spots on the line between gay and not. Let's just say she was close enough off center to be intrigued. And too scared to do anything about it, except write about it."

I went to the bookshelf and pulled out *Soft Touch* and showed my sister the ball-pointed stars. She paged through the book, looked up. "See," she said. "That's what I'm trying to tell you. Each of these stories involves two women. I think Mom regretted not going back to Adrienne, saying yes, seeing what would happen."

"Maybe she did go back, Sharon. Maybe she and Adrienne were lovers. They could have been, you know." I liked the gasp I produced. "And," I added, "our conservative father would never admit to being cuckolded by a woman, would he?"

"Damn you, Sam." Sharon stood up and put on her coat. "I was sure Mom was telling me to not live a life of regrets, to give Wilfred and me another chance."

"She did say that, Sharon, only maybe not in those stories. She wrote about you and Wilfred in the third story, where you're crazy and Wilfred is blind. Remember? Go call your husband."

She stood at the door for a long moment, then opened it and looked back. "I hate you, Sam," she said, lovingly. I put the books back on the shelf where they belonged.

I had just finished my To Do list for the next day and was brushing my teeth when I heard a knock. "Sam. . .are you there?"

"Yes," I yelled, wiping off my mouth, racing for the door

"So am I," Rose answered.

She leaped into my arms, her legs gripping my thighs, and we didn't talk for a while. Then I put clean sheets on my bed and she scooted between them and closed her eyes. "I'm exhausted, Sam. We can catch up in the morning." And we did.

Two days later, Will called to tell me that his mom and dad were going away for a week and could I come over once in a while to play with him and Enid. Han didn't speak English very well and definitely wasn't good at reading to them.

"Where are they going?" I asked. Not any of my business, maybe, or maybe it was?

"Just away. From us." Will sounded a little disappointed.

"I'll be there, buddy," I promised. "Can I bring a friend?"

"Whatever," Will answered. A little prepubescent, but not surly. He was going to be okay. Enid, too, if I could judge by her insistent "I want to talk, too" in the background and the eventual handing over of the phone to her. Then my sister came on. "I'm going off the Zoloft," she said, "and onto the next place. Mazatlan and beyond. And besides, Angie moved to Iowa and is organizing the local Elmira AA group. Life moves on."

"Yes, it does," I agreed, about to tell her about Rose's return.

But she went on, "Wilfred and I needed to make peace with our ghost, like you have, like Mom said."

Mom said that? That was my unused sermon. Is it possible that it had been channeled to each of us by a mother who continued to insist from the grave on her mother's right to preach at her children? "I'm glad," I said.

Rose brought a box of her clothes to my house. "It's easier," she explained, "since I'm only using my apartment to write in." She was working on her second novel, from the viewpoint of a young male. When she asked to see my Jack story, to get the feel of the language and all, I hesitated, but by then, I understood that no matter what Mom thought, my strengths lay in deeds not words, and

I gave her Jack. “A gift from the heart,” I said, and after she read it, she agreed. “Full of the human condition, Sam,” she said. “Also full of grammatical and spelling errors. And no ending. Does Jack just get successful as a skateboard expert and that’s it?”

“No, he gets the black-haired girl. That’s the best part,“ I answered.

CHAPTER NINETEEN

I was back to working on the iMac, Rose having commandeered the PC and taken it to her studio, as she now called her apartment, for the fifth rewrite of her first novel after an agent asked for the whole thing. I decided to clean up the computer's desktop and tossed several of my old files in the trash can. By mistake, I realized a few minutes later, and I clicked on the trash icon and rolled through the discarded stuff, looking for them. A folder appeared entitled, "Four to Go."

I called Sharon. "Mom's at it again," I said. "Come over."

My sister, tanned and calm, arrived with Krispy Kremes and coffee. She pulled up a chair next to mine and said, "Okay, I'm ready." I clicked on the folder.

RECYCLING

Blanche has her bag packed. Not literally, of course. In their small house one can't open a suitcase without the children noticing it, asking questions, Roger stumbling over it. She has listed the essentials, though, on the back of a sheet of computer paper, the other side promoting a method of penis enlargement. Roger's FAX spews out that kind of thing during the night and he retrieves the ads every morning, piles them on his desk, and uses the blank sides for downloads from the internet. Blanche frequently raids this stash for scratch paper or for the first drafts of manuscripts because she finds it difficult to edit on the screen; she needs a red pen and the ability to cross out without vaporizing her thoughts. She never knows when she might want to use them again.

So her bag is packed, in theory at least. And the house is clean, the laundry folded, the children's busy high school schedules written on the calendar in the kitchen beside the phone. All she has to do is step away from her desk, run a finger down the list, throw two bras, six panties, the rest into the bag, leave.

However, before she does that, she will write a note to explain herself. Why a woman, forty-six, with half-grown children, husband of sorts, a house, why would she will give it all up, go off on her own, begin again? She turns on her computer, sits back, waits for the words.

"I am gone and you are wondering why. You are making some guesses. I hope that the guessing is being done over dinner, the three of you. I always wanted you to talk to each other more.

"I will try to explain. Remember that children's game, a tent of fingertips touching fingertips? Close your eyes and you are

convinced that you press against a smooth strong wall, the connection tight, solid. Open your eyes and you see that it is an illusion, that your breath swirls through your widespread fingers and against your open palms like a warm breeze. Think of me like that, fingertips touching fingertips, truth flowing through the openings, between the words, never quite contained."

She gets up and pours herself a cup of coffee. Becky and Jeff are in school; Roger off to work, his forehead bent, as usual, in a frown born of anger, she supposes. At times, when he looks at her over his cereal, she believes she is the cause. The children take turns feeling responsible also, their eyebrows signaling their apprehension at his glance. Blanche doesn't know how his office staff receives the furrowed brow; it is possible Roger leaves a gaggle of guilt-infected victims behind him wherever he goes.

She won't write about the frown. She will write about the space between fingers that leaks truth despite the illusion of solid walls.

"My leaving-taking began three years ago, the day I met a person who, despite the flashing yellow lights on every cross street of our friendship, would become my love. I smiled when I thought of her; I laughed and cried when we were together. She awoke a stranger in me, a lost soul who had huddled forever behind my breastbone waiting to be found. When I was with her, my days did not slip between my fingers, but nestled for long moments in the palm of my hand."

Blanche likes the sound of that last phrase. She touches her cheek, feels Adrienne's touch, recalls how her own fingertips had responded, explored a familiar, exotic landscape. They met Tuesday afternoons at Angie's apartment.

Once they had escaped for a weekend at the beach. "Writing," she explained to her family and they believed her. She and Angie never spoke of the next place, still afloat as they were in the wonder of the now.

"Then she died."

Blanche needn't say more. Her family will remember the friend who was killed crossing a street, Blanche's monumental grief that shook the house, their days, their belief in her sanity.

When tears failed to heal the wound her life had become, Blanche turned to words. Her stories spoke of regret, what-ifs, imaginings of the barren years to come. They served as poultices, soothing the edges of pain, but not curing her.

"This is all I'll say right now: That I leave to find my Self, a cliché, I know. But you see, I almost had her in hand, this Self. I could feel her heartbeat, hear her breath. Perhaps you'll understand some day."

Blanche reads what she has written. Then she prints the paragraphs and sets them aside. She won't be able to work on them for a while, the sentences too liquid, impossible to handle so soon after writing them.

A door opens, closes. She looks at her watch. Her children are not due for three hours.

"Hi. I came home for lunch." Roger's eyes skim across her, settle on the window pane behind her. "A quick sandwich?" He passes her door, goes to the kitchen, rummages in the refrigerator. Blanche follows him, pours herself another cup of coffee and watches as he piles lunchmeat and mustard on two slices of bread, opens a Coke, sits down across from her at the table.

He takes a bite then puts the sandwich down and pushes the plate away. He wipes his mouth with a paper napkin. "I need to talk to you," he says.

She recognizes those words. She has often imagined them, rehearsed them, wallowed their mantric power, but she had never been able to say them aloud. Somehow, Roger's lips open and close upon them now, the next inexorable wave of words about to break through.

"I am suffocating." His glance, red-edged as if he has been rubbing his eyes, flits, lands between her brows. "I didn't know how stifling our life had become until I met someone with whom I can breathe. I don't expect you to understand." He clears his throat. "I'm sorry to hurt you." The speech, heartless, brave, ends. He waits.

"How can you do this?" Blanche truly wants to know. How can he be doing this, so cleanly, so sure-footedly, so grammatically, when it has taken her years of desolation to stumble to this moment?

Roger's mouth moves, each word incised into the air between them as if she is to read it, not hear it, his forehead rippling with effort. But he isn't answering her question.

"No, Roger, not why." She leans toward him, her hand wavers, lights on his hard knuckles. "How?" Afterwards, she cannot decide which frightened him most, her curiosity or her touch. Whatever the cause, he recoils, stands, flees. A moment later, his car rumbles away.

In the void following the slam of the door, Blanche contemplates her husband's abandoned sandwich. She reaches for it, remembers the thick layer of mustard, pulls her hand back.

The wave of astonishment that had swelled and crested as she listened to Roger end their marriage subsides. In its gritty backwash, she is interested to discover a meandering rivulet of a smile stirring up, and as it moves through her, a billow of laughter, a salty guffaw pooling at the base of her throat.

Blanche rinses the plate, wraps the sandwich for whichever child finds it first, goes to her desk.

As she waits for the computer to awaken, she picks up the draft of her note lying on the corner of the desk. She hesitates, finds her red pen. Crossing out, circling, underlining, a story gathers amidst the ribbons of red ink, an ironic story, the kind Adrienne had always liked. Running out of space to scribble, she turns the paper over, jots her next thought in the margins of an ad for an ointment promising "hours of unbelievable pleasure." She wonders if Roger has seen it.

"That kind of answers our questions, doesn't it?" I felt like getting drunk and headed to the kitchen.

Sharon followed me, leaned against the counter. "It's okay, Sam." She touched my shoulder, took her hand away when I shrugged under it. "She trusted us with her secret."

"I'd rather not know it." I closed the fridge door, empty-handed. Rose and I hadn't worked out the grocery thing yet. "If Mom was so smart about life and all, wouldn't she know that parents aren't supposed to reveal their secrets to their kids?"

"Kind of ruins the Madonna image you've built up, does it? The one where the saintly mother holds her son on her lap for all eternity? Whispering into his pink shell of an ear each time he squirms and wants to get down? You still believe that Mom is giving you directions from her grave."

I pointed at the computer. "So what is that?"

"It's a shove off her lap, Sam. When she died and left these stories to you, you were still nuzzling her, gripping her blue robe. She wanted you to know that she was much more than a mother, that you are a lot more than a son."

"I've never thought of myself as just a son."

"Really? When Mom died, being a son was the only thing you were doing reasonably well. Just like for years, motherhood was Mom's only job. Even her teaching was a kind of extended motherhood. Neither one of you had any alternatives to what life handed you. Then, within a couple of years, Adrienne/Angie happened, Dad departed, we grew up. What she had left were memories, her iMac, and the time to find out about the stranger inside her." Sharon reached for my arm again. "I think she wanted you to start searching way sooner than that. You have, you know."

She had learned that touch from my mother. "So, you think I've changed?" I wanted to hear her say it, to confirm what I already knew.

"You still need help," my sister answered. "Good thing you have Rose." She released me and went back to the iMac. "Mom's still here," she said.

"Wait. I'm not over the last one yet." But I went back, read over her shoulder as Sharon scrolled.

To Sam (and of course, Sharon, who stands reading over his right shoulder, as I have planned):

"For once she's got it wrong," I said.

"Be quiet."

You've read my stories by now, some of them at least, the rest vaporized by a delete button or publication in obscure anthologies.

And you are wondering why I left these to you. And why I wrote them in the first place. You've made some guesses, I hope a deux. Like my character Blanche, I always hoped you would talk to each other more.

However, my dears, I want you to know that about the time this last story was written, one of you came by, asked me how I was doing, hugged me, and I understood I was not alone, had not been alone ever. You two have always fidgeted at my side, providing grist for the mill of my days, filling them plump with joy and sorrow and laughter, even in the leanest, saddest of times. Lately, I have felt your collective hand on my thigh, just as Frank felt his daughter's.

And now I, too, give myself over to you.

Make of me and my stories what you will, but know that I think of you at this very moment, my fingertips tucked under my chin, palms touching, no illusions or cool breezes now, the warm skin of my hands a prayerful temple, thumbs pressing against my heart, fingertips reaching out, sending to you, my children, my love, my almost-peace.

Her eyes closed, hands aligned along her breastbone, the ruby ring askew on her finger, Sharon bowed her head. "Namaste, Mom," she said.

"Damn," I answered.

Sharon gave me her look. Then she grinned and stood up and touched her lips to mine.

Once more, I felt a little disappointed in that old way, and I blinked a couple of times at the iMac as I pushed the green button and let it rest.